Love Sucks!

Melissa Francis

HARPER TEEN

An Imprint of HarperCollinsPublishers

To my sons, Ian and Rader

It makes me proud to know you would fight evil vampires to protect me. And for the record, I'd do the same for you, if you'd just clean your rooms.

HarperTeen is an imprint of HarperCollins Publishers.

Love Sucks!
Copyright © 2010 by Melissa Francis
All rights reserved. Printed in the United States of America.
No part of this book may be used or reproduced in any manner whatsoever without written permission except in the case of brief quotations embodied in critical articles and reviews. For information address HarperCollins Children's Books, a division of HarperCollins Publishers, 10 East 53rd Street, New York, NY 10022.
www.harperteen.com

Library of Congress Cataloging-in-Publication Data
Francis, Melissa McKenzie.
    Love sucks! / Melissa Francis. — 1st ed.
        p.   cm.
    Summary: Eighteen-year-old vampire AJ's life and relationships become even more complicated when she is suddenly targeted by demons who threaten to destroy her family if she does not use her powers to help them find magical runes coveted by their master.
    ISBN 978-0-06-143099-2
    [1. Vampires—Fiction. 2. Stepfamilies—Fiction. 3. Interpersonal relations—Fiction. 4. Demonology—Fiction. 5. High schools—Fiction. 6. Schools—Fiction.] I. Title.
PZ7.F84685Lo 2010   2009054133
· [Fic]—dc22   CIP
                                                                                                            AC

Typography by Jennifer Rozbruch
10 11 12 13 14 LP/RRDH 10 9 8 7 6 5 4 3 2 1
❖
First edition

Chapter 1

My mother's baby shower.

Okay, this is horrifying news on many levels. First of all, I'm eighteen. (Okay, I've only been eighteen for a week, but that means I'm no longer seventeen and therefore technically I'm an adult.) I know how she got pregnant. There is no way I want to think about that, yet it seems to be all I *can* think about. And let me just say—ew. Seriously, ew.

But the whole "omigod my mom is having *the s-e-x*" thing isn't the worst part of this pregnancy debacle.

No. Did I forget to mention that my mom is a pregnant *vampire*?

Oh, and lest you think *that* is the worst part of this

mess, the father of said vampire baby is a warlock. Yeah, that's what I said—a warlock.

How very melting pot of us.

Or would that be cauldron?

But that's not all! We're like a paranormal infomercial here in Valley Springs, Mississippi. By getting pregnant, it seems my mom is fulfilling some ancient vampire prophecy. Now, you would think this would be a good thing. But no. Unfortunately, there is a big group of vampire baddies who don't want that prophecy to be fulfilled because it would seriously screw with their plans for world domination.

But guess what? We're still not to the worst part of this story.

My stepdad, the warlock who's my momma's baby daddy, is also the daddy of Ryan Fraser. The boy I'm helplessly in love with—and the boy who is now my stepbrother.

It's been five months since the big baby announcement. Five long months. In that time, I've managed to find out a lot more about the warlock side of my blended family, thanks to Ryan's aunt Doreen. I still have a lot to learn, though. Because I'm deathly afraid that if the Serpentines realize my mom is pregnant with a warlock's child, all undead hell is going to break loose.

And let me just say, I'm in no mood for vampire wars.

So as I sit in the living room of our antebellum home with two dozen of Valley Springs' finest women oohing and aahing over the sweetest little baby gifts you could ever imagine (say that in a Scarlett O'Hara voice and you'll have a pretty good picture of my current nightmare), all I seem to be able to think about is evil vampires, good warlocks, and a possible paranormal apocalypse.

Something is *really* not right with this picture.

"AJ? Did Ana and Ainsley have cheerleading tryouts today?" my mom's assistant, Laura, asked me.

Did I mention my mom is a doctor? Not just any doctor. A heart specialist. Yes, we sure know the definition of irony here in the Fraser-Ashe household.

"Yes, ma'am. They're excited about moving up from junior high. They can't wait."

"Well, I've seen them perform. They're shoo-ins, I'm sure."

I smiled. I sure hoped so. My twin sisters had never really dealt with rejection before. Of course, I couldn't imagine them *not* making it. Besides being blond and beautiful, they practiced almost twenty-four/seven. Plus, my friend Malia was one of the judges.

Yeah, they were shoo-ins.

Aunt Doreen passed me the latest opened gift—a lovely little layette in mint green with a fuzzy baby bunny on the breast. I grinned and passed the gift on to the person next to me. When would my hell be over?

Soon. Auntie Tave's voice echoed in my head. *It will be over very soon, I promise.*

I glanced at my flame-haired godmother and smiled. Tave and I had been connected since last year, when she tried to psychically find out if I had bitten a boy and turned him into a vampire. Something happened during the process, permanently keeping us linked. She can't read my thoughts exactly, but she can feel what I'm feeling. And even though she can't hear the words inside my head, I can hear hers if they're directed to me. And sometimes that's a big pain in my ass.

Being connected to Tave kinda keeps me on the straight and narrow now, because there's nothing worse than your momma's best friend being able to spy on your feelings. It's a little frustrating, actually—especially since up until a few weeks ago, I was always feeling so guilty about wanting to pull my stepbrother into my bedroom and make out with him until I couldn't breathe.

Thankfully, I had finally started to put those feelings away.

The ladies all stood, and I realized the layette was the last gift. The shower was coming to an end. Finally.

Mom looked tired, but she needed this adult time. She'd been on bed rest because of complications with the pregnancy and had been going stir-crazy.

As the crew of crooning women started their farewells, a storm of testosterone entered the room and headed straight for the remainder of the pretty lemon cake. My stepdad, Rick, and my two younger stepbrothers, Oz and Rayden, each cut themselves a slice big enough to feed a third-world country. Ryan came in shortly after and did the same.

We made eye contact, and I fought the old squiggly feeling in my belly when his dark-chocolate gaze caught mine.

"How'd the shower go, hon?" Rick asked Mom as he wrapped an arm around her growing waist and kissed her on the neck. "Did we score a bountiful booty?"

"We got lots of booties, you punny, punny man. And because I had to do all the heavy lifting of opening the gifts, you get to write the thank-you notes."

"Lucky me." He smiled again, but worry tinged his brow. "You look tired. Let's get you upstairs."

My cell phone buzzed and I checked the message.

It was a reminder that I had a prom committee meeting tomorrow. Prom was just a few weeks away, and we had no theme and no direction, and I had no date. But being on the prom committee meant I had to live *la vida prom* every day whether I liked it or not.

The kitchen door slammed open, and Ainsley called my name. Her voice was frustrated.

"AJ!"

"Living room," I said.

Ainsley's long, wheat-colored ponytail swung like a mane behind her head as she rushed into the room.

"Something's not right with Ana," she said.

"What do you mean?" Ryan asked.

Oz and Rayden stopped midchew.

"We didn't do anything," Rayden said, his eyes wide. "I swear."

Ainsley turned toward them and shook her head. "This isn't about your sad spell-casting attempt to turn her into a Sasquatch. When she woke up this morning with pit hair longer than her ponytail, Aunt D fixed her right up. But don't think she won't get y'all back. If we can find her again."

"Find her? What's going on?" I asked.

"Tryouts were today, right?" Ainsley said. "Well, we

were doing the routine we always do with the gymnastics bit? You know, with the midair acrobatics that always impresses everyone?"

I nodded, because I knew exactly what she was talking about. She and Ana had no issues using their super skills to jump just a little bit higher than everyone else or to add one extra twist or flip to their routine. It was impressive.

"Well, something went wrong. Ana didn't land well— which just isn't possible. Seriously, she's like a cat. She never misses her landings. Ever!" Ainsley said.

"Maybe she landed on a rock," Ryan offered.

Ainsley and I both shot him a *Yeah, right* look.

"Okay. Sorry. Was just trying to help," he said.

"Then what happened?" I asked.

"She was hurt. Her ankle snapped. I heard it. Of course, it was already starting to heal by the time everyone got to her. But the damage was already done. She had fallen. During *tryouts*. And everyone heard her bone crack."

"Well, Malia was there. She knows what kind of cheerleader Ana is. She'll make the team."

"That's just it. She *didn't* make the team. They wrapped her ankle, and she faked a call to Mom to take her to the doctor. But they all think her ankle is broken, which means she'd have to sit out the season. So she didn't make the team. And, of course, she's pissed."

I sighed. Poor Ana.

"She'll get over it," I said. "She'll have to."

"She's totally pouting, and she's blaming Malia," Ainsley said. "She took off after tryouts."

Rick reentered the room. "Are you talking about Ana?" he asked.

Ainsley nodded.

I sighed. "Where is she?" I asked. "Listen, I know you're communicating with her right now. Tell me where she is and I'll go get her."

"Hang on. Let me see if I can get her to tell me."

Ainsley closed her eyes and concentrated. I could see by her expression that Ana wasn't cooperating. "She's at O'Reily's farm. She was going to hide out at the Love Shack to try to cool off," she said finally.

"Okay, this is what we're going to do," Rick said. "Your mom is exhausted and doesn't need to worry about her pouting prodigal daughter. Ryan, I want you and AJ to go get her. She needs to be here by dinner."

"Can we come, too?" Oz asked.

"We don't need your help, kid," Ryan said.

"Actually, I think that's a great idea," Rick said. "I want you guys all out of the house for a while so your mom can rest. Take the minivan. All of you go and bring your sister home."

Chapter 2

We piled into the minivan. Ryan was driving, and I managed to fight off Rayden for shotgun.

The boys played their Game Boys in the back of the van as Ainsley sat quietly in the middle. She was trying to reestablish a connection with Ana, but I could tell by her facial expression she was failing. It wasn't long before Ryan was driving down the dirt road that led to the farm.

And to the memories of the incident that started the madness of my current life.

Okay, maybe that's exaggerating a little, but whatever.

"You gonna be okay going to the farm?" Ryan asked.

He always was really good at reading me.

"Yeah, I guess. I need to face my not-so-distant past eventually, right? Sometimes I wish I could have a do-over for that night. If I hadn't been so angry at you, if I hadn't gone into the woods with Noah for some revenge snogging, he'd probably still be alive."

"AJ, he might still be alive, but they would've changed someone else."

When Ryan was like this, it made it hard to remember we were no longer a couple. He always knew what to say to ease my anxiety. Longing bubbled to the surface, and I fought not to drown in it. I had worked so hard to move on. For months I had put up a good front. After everything that had happened in the fall, Ryan and Lindsey decided to give dating a real shot. So, shedding the role of girlfriend and taking on that of supportive sister, I smiled when I saw them holding hands at school and even forced myself to stop eavesdropping. Okay, I *tried* to stop eavesdropping. What's the point of having super skills if you can't use them sometimes?

I'm not sure exactly when it happened, but a few weeks ago I realized I was no longer faking it. It was bizarre. I walked in on Ryan kissing Lindsey good night. As usual, I mentally braced myself for the normal eruption of ugly green flames to consume me—and nothing happened. No lump in my throat, no revved-up heart rate, no curdled stomach, and no poisonous anger.

Nothing but a twinge of sadness that I imagine won't go away for a long time.

What a relief it was to realize that I finally was moving on. Now, if I could just find a date for the prom. Oh well, a girl must tackle one teenage emotional crisis at a time, I guess.

Even though the trees lining the gravel road were showing their first signs of spring, I didn't feel that blooming sense of hope that usually comes with the season. Instead, my stomach knotted when the farm came into sight. Smoke plumed from the chimney of the main house, hovering above the green rooftop in the distance, while cows grazed in the pasture between the house and the woods.

But even the postcardlike scenery didn't warm me up to the idea of returning to the farm.

"Any luck?" I asked Ainsley.

"She just got to the cabin, but she couldn't go in because someone was already there."

The "cabin" was the original farmhouse located in the back of the O'Reily property. It had been abandoned for years and was known by the kids as the Love Shack. Even though O'Reily's farm was private property, kids often snuck out to the dilapidated building to do dirty deeds. Like make out. Or get drunk. Or get high. Or all of the above.

"Wow. Seems a little early for a party," Ryan said.

"Shit," Ainsley said, her tone pitching up an octave. "AJ, it's not a party. It's Mr. Charles! He's at the cabin!"

Ryan put the pedal to the metal, spitting gravel as he tore off down the road. We weren't far from the farm, but it would take a little bit to get to the Love Shack because we had to walk to it.

My phone rang.

"What's wrong?" Auntie Tave asked.

"Tave, this is getting old," I said, unable to hide my frustration. "I know you mean well, but can't I keep one emotion to myself?"

"Sorry, hon. Your mood changed so suddenly, it made my heart stop. What happened?"

"Nothing for you to worry about," I lied. "Ana didn't make the squad, and she's off pouting at O'Reily's. Rick sent us after her so Mom could rest after today's shower."

"Tell her," Ryan said. "She needs to know. She'll know

something's up anyway if you come in contact with him, so tell her."

I sighed. He was right. "Tave? Ana saw Mr. Charles at O'Reily's farm."

"I'm on my way."

Ryan slammed the van into park as we pulled up to the double gate at the far end of the farm. The property was lined by a white wooden fence, and from here the main house looked tiny. We all climbed the gate and landed with a loud clunk on the metal cattle guard.

"Stick together," Ryan said. "We don't wanna give that psycho a chance to grab one of us again. Strength in numbers."

"Shhh. Did you hear that?" I asked. I closed my eyes and concentrated, sharpening my super hearing.

And that's when a bloodcurdling scream pierced my ears.

"Ana!" I yelled. "Where are you? We're coming!"

We all took off in a panic for the woods. We ran about fifty feet before we heard another scream. But this one wasn't Ana—it was more like the roar of a wild animal, and it stopped us dead in our tracks. The sound was high-pitched and eerie. It vibrated into my bones and made me want to curl up into a fetal position and cry out for Mommy. For the first time, I truly understood the definition of *bloodcurdling*.

"What the hell was that?" Ryan asked.

"It's some kind of demon," Ainsley squeaked. "And it's chasing Ana. She's gone invisible and has jumped up in a tree. It's lost track of her but is starting to sniff up the trees to find her. We've got to help."

"We need to wait on Auntie Tave," Ryan said. "She'll know what to do."

"That's my sister, Ryan! We don't have time to wait!" I yelled, taking off for the trees.

What's happening? Tave's voice rang in my head. *Are you okay?*

The only way for me to respond to Tave was with my emotions. She couldn't hear my thoughts, but she could feel what I was feeling. Normally I would try to calm down so as not to worry her, but there was so much adrenaline and anxiety pumping through me right now that there was no way I could chill. Besides, something told me I might need some adult supervision.

Ever since Mr. Charles kidnapped me in the fall, I'd kinda sorta been fantasizing about fanging him into oblivion.

Probably not a good idea, but damn if it didn't sound fun.

"Ana!" I called again once I entered the woods. "Where are you?"

I slowed down to listen for her and to look for Mr. C. A couple of tree branches cracked above, startling me. I looked up, and that's when I saw what had Ana on the run.

Ainsley was right—it was a demon. And by the looks of its fangs, it wasn't just any old demon—it was a vampire demon.

Ana was obviously still invisible, but I could hear her panting. And if I could hear her, I'm sure the demon could, too. It was only a matter of time before it found her.

And then what?

"Hey! You!" I yelled. The demon stopped climbing the tree and glanced at me. Its eyes sparked red for a brief moment, and I'm pretty sure it licked its lips.

"Damn, you're a big bucket of ugly. Why don't you pick on someone your own size?" My voice was strong and I sounded tough, but I was shaking on my inside parts. It wasn't easy trying to bully a bully. Especially one as big, ugly, and supernatural as this one.

I saw another tree shake and knew I had bought enough time for Ana to put more distance between her and Mr. Hyde up there.

The demon thing roared again and dove from the tree toward me, a cloud of gray smoke following in its wake. From the ground, it looked only as big as a tall adult, but as it was plummeting toward me I realized it was huge and as wide as a Mack truck. It looked part gorilla, part human, with long arms and a giant head. It was kinda like a furless Sasquatch with fangs.

Fangs that were bigger than any I had ever seen.

My feet seemed glued to the ground. I needed to move, levitate, run, jump—something, but all I was able to do was stand still while panic burned my throat.

The demon landed just a few feet away from me. Its eyes were the color of caramel, but they glowed bright like lights.

"Now that you're here, I don't need your sister. You're the one that we want," it said in a gravelly voice, like Kathleen Turner after too many cigarettes. Its breath was hot and strangely sweet, like bubblegum, and I was overwhelmed with a sudden need to vomit.

The air turned to static and began to crackle. The demon bared its fangs as it wrapped its meaty fingers around my wrist and pulled me into its chest.

"We need to have a serious discussion about your manners and your lack of dental hygiene," I said.

17

The monster yanked my arm harder, nearly popping it out of the socket, and that's when a big blue electric ball flew over my head and hit the demon in the shoulder. It howled in pain, giving me the time I needed to escape. Ryan stood a few feet away, blue sparks shooting from his fingertips. The kids stood behind him, both boys primed to cast their own spell, with Ainsley baring her fangs.

"Run!" I screamed.

Ainsley and the boys turned to run, but they didn't get very far. Mr. Charles appeared from behind a tree and grabbed Oz by the scruff of his neck.

"How about you stay put," he said with a sneer. "AJ, we won't hurt the kids if you'll just come with us."

"Dude, not all blondes are dumb."

Mr. Charles looked the same, with mossy green eyes and short dark hair. I used to think he was sex on a stick, but I was no longer hot for teacher.

"You know, if you had just cooperated last time, none of this would be happening. And I would be a vampire."

I rolled my eyes as the demon regained its composure and started to circle me. Where the hell was Auntie Tave? Mr. C. we could handle, but this monster thing? I was clueless.

"If you believe they're ever going to make you a

vampire, you're dumber than you look."

The demon was still circling me, but it was eyeing Ryan like he would be tasty on a Triscuit. I had no idea where Ana was, but for the time being it seemed she was out of harm's way.

"What do you want with me?" I asked, trying to distract it from eating one of my siblings as a Scooby snack.

"You're the key holder, which means without you, the runes can't be found," the demon growled in a raspy voice. "Besides, you're one of us, AJ. You can deny your history all you want, but that doesn't change that you're Serpentine. You'll embrace it one day. You'll see." Its scratchy voice hurt my ears like squeaky Styrofoam.

Ryan quickly nodded at me, telling me to keep the demon talking. He closed his eyes and his lips began to move.

"I'm not full-blooded Serpentine. My blood is dirty, remember?"

"Yes, well, we've seen . . . the error in our ways. It never occurred to us that the key holder wouldn't be full-blooded. But you and your sisters will be welcomed home with open arms."

"Thanks for the offer, but we'll pass."

"Your sisters have that choice. You don't."

The overly sweet smell of the demon's breath was beginning to make me sick. The creature circled to my left and I slid to the right. Oz stood stoic in Mr. Charles's grip, and Ainsley had moved next to Ryan. By the deep look of concentration on her face, I could tell she was still in contact with Ana.

I glanced at Ryan. He opened his eyes and raised his eyebrows. Whatever he had planned, he was ready.

"I found out last year there's always a choice," I said to the demon.

"Yes, but you must live with the consequences. For instance, if you come with me willingly, then we won't hurt that half-breed baby or your mother. If you don't come with me, then you leave us no choice."

Its words startled me, and I stopped moving just long enough for it to pounce. It wrapped its arm around my waist and began climbing the pine tree like it was a monkey.

I bared my fangs with every intention of sucking the beast dry—when another blue globe hit the demon in the back. It yelped like a wounded animal as its body stiffened.

In its paralyzed state, it lost its hold on me. I tried to focus quickly, hoping I could pull off a quick levitation, but no luck. I landed with a snap at the base of the tree. Pain radiated through my hips and into my back.

Mr. Charles took off running, dragging Oz behind him. But Oz was a clever little thing and managed a quick spell. He clapped his hands together, then touched Mr. C's arm. Mr. Charles squealed like a little girl as giant green boils began popping up on his arm, quickly moving to his neck, then his face.

Oz couldn't stifle a giggle as he broke free and ran toward the cow pasture.

"Can you run?" Ryan asked me.

"No. Landed on my hip. It cracked and hasn't started healing yet. You go, get the kids out of here. I'll figure something out."

"Yeah, right." He leaned over and scooped me up like I was a feather pillow. "We've only got a few minutes. That was a half-assed paralyzer spell, but I didn't know what else to do."

Ryan tore through the woods. I was in awe of how easily he maneuvered through the branches and over protruding roots as he carried me.

As we reached pasture, I was relieved to see Auntie Tave and Aunt Doreen. But that relief was short-lived as that sickly sweet smell hit me again. I looked over Ryan's shoulder to see the demon just a few yards away.

"Ryan, it's back!"

It roared and dove right for us, knocking Ryan to the ground. He didn't let go of me as he twisted his body to absorb the shock of the fall. The demon reared back and swiped at my face with a meaty claw. I threw my good leg up, kicking its arm away and saving my face from a nasty gash.

I did not, however, save my leg.

The claws tore through my jeans like they were paper; the wound burned like a blue flame. I rolled out of Ryan's arms as he began to mutter, but the demon was too quick. It swooped down and picked Ryan up by the legs, flinging him into the air toward a tree.

"Ryan!" I screamed.

All of a sudden, a flash of brilliant white light blinded me. When I opened my eyes, Ryan was suspended in mid-air, about five feet from smashing into a tree.

"Wee nasty beast, I'll send ye back tae hell where ye came from," Aunt Doreen said, raising her hands above her head.

A loud, earsplitting groan of disappointment pierced the air as the demon realized he had been bested. Aunt D quickened her unintelligible mumbo jumbo, but just as she cast her spell, the demon shot back into the woods. We heard one last yelp as it disappeared.

"At least I hit the bloody thing. Maybe it'll walk with a limp for a while."

"Where's Mr. Charles? Don't tell me he got away," I moaned.

"Aye, I saw the pustule-covered coward slinking off when the demon attacked Ryan. Oz, ye get dessert first tonight for casting that spell. Brilliant, laddie!"

"Um, a little help here?" Ryan said. "As much as I appreciate not being a pine-tree pancake, this being frozen in midair thing really isn't all that comfortable."

"Och, sorry Ryan." Aunt D worked her magic and Ryan floated safely to the ground.

Ryan walked over and scooped me into his arms again. "How's your leg?"

"Burns, but I can manage."

"Some things never change," he said with a sad smile that made my heart flutter. "You'll always be the same stubborn AJ." He pushed a strand of hair behind my ear, then carried me to the van. After I was settled into the front seat, Auntie Tave came over to talk to me.

"I'm very proud of you, honey. You were so brave. But you need more training than I can give you."

"What *was* that? A hairless King Kong Jr.?"

"It's called a Bborim. It's a shape-shifting demon that is also part Serpentine. They are vile beasts and dangerous. Family meeting when we get home."

Chapter 3

As soon as we arrived home, Aunt Doreen took over. "We can talk at dinner. Mum is still resting and we dinna want to wake her just to stress her more, ye ken? Kids, get to your homework. AJ, come here and let me tend to your leg."

I sat down at the island in the kitchen, and Ryan brought me a hemoshake. Aunt D pulled out her emergency medical kit, full of homemade salves and herbs and other things that were better left unidentified.

My cracked hip was fine now, but for some reason the wound on my leg had barely started healing. "I must need some extra hemoglobin, because this stupid gash on my leg still burns like a bitch," I said.

"That's the demon's curse," Aunt Doreen said. "Or I suppose they consider it a gift—but to their enemies, 'tis definitely a curse. One reason a Bborim is so difficult to defeat is because the injuries they inflict inhibit your natural immunity. Vampires who canna regenerate quickly make for easier targets."

She clapped her hands twice and the kitchen stereo came on. Aunt Doreen immediately began to buzz around the kitchen singing.

"Is that the Bee Gees?" I asked.

"Aye. I've been around a long time now, but nothin' stirs my soul more than the Bee Gees. Except for maybe ABBA. And Elvis. Och! I loved that man."

I cocked an eyebrow and Ryan laughed. Who knew?

"Now off with ye, and we'll talk more at dinner, aye?"

Ryan and I left the kitchen together. My leg was starting to heal, but there was no hope for my jeans.

"Guess I should go upstairs to change."

"Yeah, those jeans have seen better days," Ryan said.

I took one stair and paused, turning to face Ryan. "Thank you for today. You've saved me twice now. This is starting to become a habit."

"One more time and I get my vampire-saving merit badge in the warlock scouts. It's always been a goal of mine, so thanks for helping me out," he said with a wink.

"Shut up, goofy," I said, ignoring the tickle in my belly as I headed upstairs to my room.

Ryan followed me. "Why do you think they want to find the runes?" he asked.

I opened the door to my bedroom and my white cat, Spike, stood from his spot on the bed and stretched. I walked over to him and scratched his head as I thought about Ryan's question.

"Remember that book Jill sent me when I was doing all that Serpentine research in the fall? Well, there was a theory that the runes were a time-traveling device. That the Frieceadans had taken and hidden the runes, then fled from the Serpentines."

"What did the Serpentines want with them?"

"According to the book, they wanted to 'correct their mistakes' and start over. They had planned to go back, form the alliance with the Frieceadans, and then betray them, annihilating your entire clan. It would be easier to go back in time when the Frieceadans lived in the open, as opposed to now where y'all are in hiding, spread out all over the globe."

"And that's their plan now?"

"I don't know. I'm just guessing. I mean, they obviously know Mom is carrying a vampire-warlock baby, and that probably terrifies them. We've kept Mom well protected, and so far the Serpentines haven't tried to get to them. But if that baby is the prophesied child I read about last year, then its blood is the anti-venom to the Serpentine bite. That will make their bite powerless, which will in turn make *them* powerless. I think they want the runes as backup. They're going to try to use me to get to the baby, and if that doesn't work, then they'll just go back in time and start over."

"What if the runes aren't the backup plan?" Ryan asked.

"What do you mean?"

"If the runes are really a time-traveling device, then think about the power they would have if they had control of them. I don't think the runes are the backup plan at all. I think they plan to go back in time and rewrite history. If we don't exist, then the baby will never be born."

"If that's true, then they want me to help them kill off my own family. Why would I do that?"

"I don't know, but they think you will. Man, Ashe, that's some family tree you've got there," Ryan joked. But his eyes weren't smiling.

"I guess it's a good thing I'm not my father's daughter then, isn't it?"

The family sat in the dining room. Our table was giant and round; we often joked it was a replica of King Arthur's round table. Rick could totally be King A, too. He was sorta majestic in his place. And even in her weakened state, Mom was definitely his queen—only without all that infidelity stuff.

Tonight's dinner was bangers and mash, and everyone seemed very happy. Auntie Tave joined us, which surprised Mom, but she was all smiles as Tave entertained us with blood-bank stories throughout dinner.

Dessert was a fabulous lemon cake that Aunt D whipped up without even blinking an eye. I know the woman is a witch, but really, not even magic could explain the depth of goodness that was her desserts.

As we all silently enjoyed our lemony slice of heaven, Aunt D took command of the table.

"We have a wee problem," she said, standing. "Here, love, ye'll need this." She walked over to Rick and poured him two fingers of scotch, neat.

"Me too," Tave said.

Aunt D nodded and poured Tave a glass. "Me three,"

she said, pouring her own serving.

"Today the bairns were chased by a beastie known as a Bborim. It was big and mean and hell-bent on taking our AJ with it back to the Serpentines."

"AJ!" Mom said, bolting from her seat. "Why didn't you tell me?"

"Have ye some tea, Mum," Aunt Doreen said, pouring her a cup of something hot. I'm quite sure it was a very special pot of tea. Mom would be calm in no time.

"We told the kids to stay quiet until tonight," Tave said, taking a very big drink of her scotch. "You're already under a lot of stress, and we didn't want to make matters worse."

"These are my children!" Mom said. "If it pertains to them, I need to know!"

"And we're telling you now," Rick said, laying a hand on her belly. "This is your child, too, and any stress could cause more problems. We aren't excluding you, but we aren't going to wake you up just to upset you."

This seemed to calm Momma down a little bit. "Okay, but don't ever think I'm too weak to know what's going on in their lives," she admonished before sitting back down and taking a sip of her tea.

"There's more," Aunt Doreen said. "As much as I wished Ryan had sent that no-good teacher of theirs to a parallel universe—preferably one with starved teacher-eating giants—I knew that was too much to ask for. Mr. Charles was also there.

"According to Ana, there was a third person who the rest of us never saw. He was in robes, and the demon and teacher both called him Elder. I'm sure he's the one who's in control of the demon right now and is probably behind this whole mess.

"We know they're after AJ because they think she's the one chance they have of retrieving the runes. We also know that they know you are carrying a half-Frieceadan, half-vampire baby and they don't like it. Mum, from now on you don't get to leave the house without a protection spell and without one of us with you."

Mom nodded. Her clear blue eyes were cloudy all of a sudden. Her forehead was drawn, and all the color had drained from her face.

"Kids, you guys will always travel in pairs," Rick added. "We're not leaving this house unprotected or alone. Am I clear?"

Aunt Doreen walked to an antique bookshelf in the living room . She pulled out a large, ancient, leather-bound book and laid it on the table in front of us as she flipped through the pages.

Each page was filled with sketches, drawings, diagrams, and calligraphy.

"Ah, yes. Here is the creature. A Bborim is a shapeshifting demon. Serpentines don't just let anyone in their inner circle, so my guess is this demon is probably part Serpentine as well."

"How could it be *part* Serpentine?" Ryan asked. "I thought they only wanted pure blood in their family."

"During the wars, the Serpentines decided the demons would be more powerful allies if they were assimilated into the clan. So they began to bite them and transform them. A Bborim that has been transformed is difficult to detect. They shapeshift into whatever they fed off last—human or animal, it doesna matter. Once they've shifted, they can maintain that form for as long as necessary.

"There are some documented cases of successful matings between the vampires and the demons, but the clan wasn't always happy with the end result. The Serpentines wanted a stronger being, and they wanted to maintain their 'superior' bloodline. In their minds they couldn't remain superior if they continued to transform Bborims. So they began to experiment with different ways to combine the two species. Eventually they developed a vaccine from the Bborim spinal fluid and marrow. When this vaccine is injected into the vampire, they become a perfect mix of the two beings."

Aunt Doreen paused and looked directly into Ryan's eyes. I had never seen her so serious before.

"The Serpentines werena always bad. They were allies of the Frieceadans. We trusted them. It's always been best if the magical folk stick together. And it was all well and good until they became power hungry. That's when the runes and the scrolls were hidden. To keep them safe from the evil that had taken over."

"And that's when the Frieceadans went into hiding?" I asked.

"Precisely. As soon as the documents were hidden, the new people in charge of the clan killed everyone involved. Including their families. They came after the Frieceadans, and they managed to kill off a good number of our people before we escaped."

"Why do you think this demon is part Serpentine?" Oz asked.

"Because it wants to take AJ back to the clan," Ryan answered.

Oz's eyes widened.

"Don't worry, kiddo. I'm not going anywhere," I said. "What makes the Bborim so dangerous, Aunt D? Why is it different from just a normal vamp?"

"One thing is, they dinna have to feed often. They're sturdy and dangerous creatures because they are difficult to sense."

"Except for that awful sweet smell," I said with a shudder. "That was like candy-store overload."

"What smell?" Rayden asked.

"You didn't smell its super-sweet breath?" I asked.

Everyone shook their heads no.

"Well, I wouldn't recommend getting close enough to smell it, because it is *nasty*."

"The Serpentines are slime. We should do to them what they tried to do to us," Ryan spat.

I flinched with every venom-tinged word.

"I'm sorry," he said when he realized how hateful he'd sounded. "I don't mean y'all. But that extended family of yours is bad with a capital B."

"Ryan!" Rick said. "The Frieceadans protect and defend. That's our place in this world. We don't bring harm to others."

Ryan stood and walked to the doorway, unable to hide the sadness on his face. "I know that, Dad. I do. I love our family and I know that the girls would never do anything intentionally to hurt us. But what if . . ." His voice trailed off.

"What if what?" I asked softly.

He looked at me and my breath hitched. "The Bborim was convinced you'd find your way home to the Serpentines. What if it was right? What if that's your destiny?" His voice was almost a whisper. "What if . . . ?"

He didn't finish the thought; he just turned away from us and walked out the door. Aunt Doreen sat next to me, hugging me close to her. "Dinna fash yerself over that lad, dearie. He's got the weight of the world on his shoulders, as do you. In the end, family will stick together. Ye'll see."

Wasn't that exactly what Ryan was worried about? Was it possible that I might one day decide the Serpentines were my real family?

Chapter 4

I spent the night dreaming of soulful brown eyes and big demon baddies. I spent the morning trying to get Tave out of my head. Now that she knew Mr. Charles was back, it seemed I couldn't get rid of her. When I finally managed to reroute my emotions, my cell phone rang.

"Honey, I know it isn't fair that I'm so tapped into you, but I can't help you protect the family if you don't help me."

"I know you mean well, Auntie Tave, but this isn't about the demon. Please, could you try to stay out of my head? It would be very helpful to my teenage state of mind if you didn't know every time I looked at Ryan and wished things were different."

Okay, so that was me fudging things a bit. I didn't want her worrying about how much I was worrying, so I figured I'd make her think my sudden emotional change was over Ryan. It must've worked, because she paused, then said, "I see. I'm so sorry, sweetie."

"It's fine. Listen, I'm running late. Can we talk later?" *Much later.*

I glanced at my reflection one last time. Tattered jeans, T-shirt, flip-flops, and hair pulled into a ponytail at the nape of my neck. Perfect girl next door. Not a hint of vampire anywhere.

Except for the backward "S" birthmark on my neck. I slid the band out of my hair and shook my ponytail free. It may be a birthmark to the world, but to me it represented ugliness, and death, and a family history that I'd like to ignore.

A history that apparently Ryan was having a hard time dealing with, I thought as I rounded the corner from the stairs to the kitchen. Ryan was sitting on a barstool at the island, eating some freshly baked bread.

I used to joke that his eyes were like a Sharpie to my soul—each time he looked at me, he left a permanent mark.

But this time, when his gaze met mine, the mark he left didn't fill me with warm fuzzies and longing. It left me sad. And empty. I tried to shake it off, but the lingering chill was bone deep. Almost exactly like my birthmark made me feel.

What was he thinking?

"Hello, dearie." Aunt Doreen bustled past Ryan and swatted him on the head. "Ye've eaten enough to feed an entire castle. Get ye away."

Ryan reluctantly moved. He picked up his backpack, then called out, "First bus is leaving—who's coming?"

A stampede of teenage feet pounded down the stairs. Ana and Ainsley rushed to the carport door and almost made it outside, but Mom's voice stopped them in their tracks.

"Ana, you're forgetting your crutches. Use them," she said from the doorway.

"Mrs. Fraser, get back to the bed. I'll take care of the weans. Dinna make things worse for the baby."

"Mooooom," Ana whined. "My ankle is fine."

"I know that, and you know that, but how are you going to explain it to everyone who heard the bone pop?"

Ana huffed a loud, angsty breath. "Fine. But I'm telling everyone it was just a sprain." She shot me a look.

"And you can tell that bitch friend of yours that I will not forgive her. She could've fought for me."

"Ana!" Mom chastised. "I know you're hurt, but you need to watch yourself. Do you hear me?"

Ana stomped back upstairs to retrieve the crutches. Mom sighed. "You okay today?" she asked me.

Her Spidey-sense must have been on full alert. "I'm good. Just didn't sleep well."

"Are you still having the dreams? I thought Aunt D's protection spells had helped."

"They're not coming as often or as strong, but they've never stopped. And there's nothing new in them for you to worry about." I walked over to Mom, rubbed her belly, and kissed her on the cheek. "Go back to bed, Momma."

"Everyone's a mother nowadays," she said with a smile. "I was serious yesterday. Don't think about keeping me out of the loop in order to protect me. I want to know everything that's going on."

"Yes, ma'am," I said. I couldn't promise, but I would sure try.

Ana stomped back down the stairs with her ankle wrapped in an Ace bandage. She dragged the crutches behind her, allowing them to bang loudly on each stair as she descended.

"Ana, quit being a baby," Mom said. "Seriously, just get over it. Sometimes this stuff just happens."

She rolled her eyes. "Whatever. AJ, can you take me to school? Ryan left without me."

"Sure. Let's go."

She was still pouting when we got into the car.

"Ana, you're going to have to let this go. You can try out again next year. Or maybe you can talk to them about being an alternate when your ankle heals."

She just stared out the window, ignoring my attempt to sway her from pouting. We rode in silence for a few minutes. About three blocks from her school, she sighed.

"What are we going to do about this Bborim thing?" she asked. "We can't let it get to Mom, and we can't let it find the runes."

"I'm not sure what to do," I answered honestly.

"I am: Find the runes before they do," Ana replied.

"Yeah. But where do we start looking? That's the question."

I pulled into the car-pool line and waited while Ana gathered her stuff. She looked like she was performing sketch comedy as she fumbled with her backpack and crutches. I tried not to laugh because I knew it would only make things worse for her mood, but seriously, it would've taken the restraint of God to stop me from giggling.

Ana glared at me. After a little more struggling, she finally got her backpack in place and the crutches under her arms. "Bite me, AJ," she said as she hobbled off.

As I pulled away from the curb, a lanky boy with dark hair and a gangly walk stopped Ana, taking her backpack from her. Ana's blush was so warm, I could feel it in the car. Maybe this ankle thing would work to her advantage.

I arrived at my school, parked in BFE, and made the three-day journey to my locker. I hated being late.

Malia and Bridget were both waiting for me. The tension between them was so thick, it felt like walking through a spiderweb. I wished they would just bury the hatchet already. You would think they'd have been able to make peace after last semester, but no can do.

"Hey, sorry I'm late. I had to run Ana to school because Ryan bolted this morning."

"He must've been in a hurry to get to Bridget's house and give her a ride," Malia snapped. Lately she had been relentless with her sniping toward Bridget. It was beginning to get old.

Bridget's eyes went wide. "*Not* what happened. If you would just bother to ask instead of assume . . ."

"Ryan picked you up?" I asked.

"Yeah, I had to take my car in to be serviced this morning. He saw me walking to school and picked me up."

Malia snorted. "I think you're the one needing servicing."

Bridget shot Malia the finger. "Whatever, Malia. Listen, I gotta go. I'll see you at lunch?" Bridget asked me.

"No. I have prom committee meeting. We still don't have a theme, and prom is in two weeks. We're choosing today, no matter what."

"Okay, call me later then." Bridget slid a glance at Malia, turned, and walked away.

"I'm telling you, something's going on with her and Ryan. I've seen them together a bunch of times now, AJ."

"Malia, nothing's going on. I promise. Bridget is way too wrapped up in Grady. You really need to just let it go. I love you both, so stop with this pettiness," I said as the first bell rang. "Crap, I gotta run. See you second period."

The morning went by fairly fast. Even Mrs. Crandall wasn't as crabby as usual. Ryan nodded and said hello when I walked in, but he seemed distant, like he was trying to sort something out about me.

It was fourth period and time to face another hour with Ryan. History used to be Mr. Charles's class. Our new teacher was Mrs. Christopher, Sheriff Christopher's wife. Her family is one of Valley Springs' founding families. We were studying the history of our town, and if anyone knew the history of this town, it was Sarah Christopher.

"How many of you know about Valley Springs' ties to Salem, Massachusetts, and the witch trials?"

I looked around. Nobody raised a hand.

"Well, that's just sad. It's the most important part of our history."

Ryan raised his hand. "How could Valley Springs be connected to the witch trials? The area that is now Mississippi was largely unexplored then, and aside from the Native Americans it was pretty much uninhabited. We didn't even become an official territory until a hundred years after the witch trials."

Mrs. Christopher beamed. "Very good, Ryan. You know your history well. But the history I'm going to discuss isn't from a textbook. It's what has been passed down from family to family over the years and is now available in the archives at the library. And, Ryan, the area wasn't uninhabited. The founding members of Valley Springs were the first Europeans in the area, and they lived in peace among the Chickasaws."

She pulled out a large book, which looked similar to the one Aunt Doreen used to look up the information on the Bborim. "I've made some copies of the applicable pages for y'all. Take one and pass it back," she said, handing stacks of stapled papers to the front row.

I flipped through the pages. They were indeed very similar to Aunt Doreen's book—lots of handwritten notes, sketches, recipes, and information about the area and the natives.

"You all know about the Salem witch hunts that started in 1692 when three Puritan girls began to act erratically and claimed they were being pricked by invisible pins. When no physical evidence of any ailment was found, the rumblings of witchcraft began to make their way through the village until finally three women were arrested.

"Those three women were not witches. However, within a day's walk of Salem, there was a small, mostly Scottish, settlement of holistic people. They lived quietly and peacefully with the natives. The Puritans were frightened of them because they did not understand their use of herbs, crystals, and metals. They were also labeled witches.

"And they *were* witches in the sense that they believed

in the use of magic, potions, spells. They really weren't that different from the Native Americans. Anyway, once innocent people were being accused in Salem, they knew it wouldn't be long before the Puritans hunted them down as well. So they made their way south."

"Wait a minute, Mrs. Christopher. If they were really witches, why did they bother leavin'? Couldn't they have just done some magic woo-woo and escaped?" Hank Fellows asked.

Mrs. Christopher laughed. "Very astute, Hank. And yes, I suppose if they really were magical in the 'woo-woo' sense, they could've escaped unharmed. But if that had happened, would the witch hunts have ever ended? If they had stayed and escaped their punishment, then an innumerable number of innocent people would've lost their lives as a direct result. This was not the first time they had to run. On page two of your handouts, you'll see that they came to America to escape persecution by another group of people they had once been allied with."

I looked up at Ryan. He briefly made eye contact, then looked back at his handout, his face a little ashen. This was hitting a little too close to home for him.

Cathy Ledbetter raised her hand. "My momma says that witches are from the devil. She's not gonna take too kindly to you spreadin' the word of the devil, Mrs. Christopher."

"I'm teaching the history of our town, Cathy, and nothing else. Now, where were we? Okay, the settlers left in the middle of the night sometime before the trials began. They needed to get far away from the puritanical arm of the church. They followed the rivers, preferring to make their home near a water source, until finally they settled in Mississippi."

Cathy raised her hand again. "Why isn't any of this in the history books? Why is it that only you have this information? Are you a witch?"

Mrs. Christopher sighed. "Cathy, as I said, this information is available at the public library and it has been verified by a historian. There are loads of artifacts on display in the library as well that verify this information. And no, I'm not a witch, but yes, some of my ancestors were practicing witches. Now, can we continue?"

Surprised murmurs spread over the classroom. It wasn't every day that a teacher admitted to having witches in her family tree.

"Who were the people they ran from the first time?" Hank asked. "Maybe our founders were really just bad guys who kept pissin' everyone off around them?"

"Well, we're not sure exactly. Many of those pages have been removed from the books. We've seen the word 'dichampyr' here and there, but nobody can translate that. We've read several references to serpents, so we know they felt double-crossed. And there is one mention of blood-suckers, but the reference is so vague, we haven't really been able to determine what they meant. So we're having to piece together a lot of the history based on notes here and there, since so many pages are missing."

I flipped through my handout and stifled a gasp. There, in black and white, was the Serpentine "S." Next to it were different places on the body the "S" had been spotted, and other variations of the mark.

Boy, was I glad I took that ponytail down this morning.

I self-consciously lifted my hand to my neck and made sure the mark was hidden. Sure, everybody had seen it by now, but maybe nobody in this class had ever—

"Hey, AJ! That looks like your birthmark! You some kinda descendant of those dichamp-whatevers?"

Heat burned my cheeks. I laughed nervously. "Guilty."

The class chuckled. Mrs. Christopher winked. I glanced at Ryan as he stoically stared straight ahead. His face was even grayer than earlier.

"I'm assigning a project that's due in two weeks. I want each of you to research your family history or ties to Valley Springs. If you're new to the area, come see me after class and I'll assign you a family to research. You can do a family tree, a report, charts, whatever you want. The specifics of the assignment are on the last page of the handouts."

When the bell rang, I nearly peed my pants in relief. I had loaded up my backpack and started toward the door when Lindsey's best friend, Meredith, stopped me. "AJ! Oh my God! I have the best idea for prom! C'mon! I can't wait to tell the committee!"

If I were to gauge her idea by exclamation marks, I'd guess we had a winner. At least, I hoped it was a winner. I was sick of trying to figure out a theme . . . especially since we should have decided on one more than a month ago.

"I can't wait to hear it."

Chapter 5

O h, hell no. *Hell* no. That ain't happenin'. Nope. Sorry. No way, no how. Cannot allow this idea to go any further.

Meredith had the entire committee's undivided attention as she told them about what we had just learned from Mrs. Christopher. She showed them her handouts, talked about the witch settlers and the bloodsuckers, and even had the nerve to turn to the page that had the Serpentine "S" and told the story about Hank "outing" me as a "dichamp-whatever."

I had to fight the urge to correct her. I mean, I'm not a dichampyr. I'm a vampire—I was born this way, not created. Of course, since people thought vampires didn't really exist, correcting her wasn't really an option.

"So, I was thinking, we should have a kind of *Twilight* meets Harry Potter prom. We could have so much fun with that! What do y'all think?"

To my horror, every girl on the committee squeed. (Why do people squee? Seriously.)

"That's kind of lame, don't you think?" I said. "I mean, both are *so over*. Like way over. In twenty years, we'll look back at our prom pictures and think, *WTF?*" *Please let them buy it. Please let them buy it.*

"Well, I think this is the perfect way to honor the history of our town and to have a little fun. Plus, the whole purpose of high school is to ask WTF? in twenty years. My mom does it all the time. C'mon! This would be hysterical—magic wands, vampire teeth, backward-*S*-shaped birthmarks. . . . We need a fun theme, something like Magically Delicious."

Magically Delicious? As a way to describe Ryan, definitely. As a prom theme? Negatory. The committee began to mumble in agreement, and I knew I was about to be outvoted. I really, really, really didn't want to go this route. It hit way too close to home for our family. And even though nobody knew about us, I couldn't help but feel this was a very bad idea. But I could also tell it was a losing battle. If we were going to go with this theme, then I was going to control the direction. Maybe it would make it easier for us in the end.

"Magically Delicious is a bowl of Lucky Charms. We should do a leprechaun thing instead."

Everyone rolled their eyes.

"How about Love Sucks?" Meredith suggested. "Maybe we could play on the star-crossed lovers thing? Warring families, a vampire falls for a witch? It'll be *Romeo and Juliet* meets Harry Potter meets *Twilight*."

"I love it!" Margaret Moore exclaimed.

"That's brilliant! Absolutely brilliant," Tammy Peters said.

I swallowed hard. I had a very bad feeling about this.

"I'll talk to Mrs. Christopher and get this approved," Meredith said. "And then we can get started with the planning. This is gonna be awesome!"

I'm glad somebody thought so.

I was barely through the kitchen door before Ryan grabbed me and pulled me back outside.

"Tree house," he grumbled.

Ryan's mood surrounded him like a thick fog. It wasn't anger, exactly, but frustration definitely tinged his aura. I could practically smell it and taste it with every breath I took.

I climbed in first, and my breath caught in my throat. I hadn't been up here since the wedding. Too many memories of stolen kisses and whispered secrets lingered everywhere. I had done a pretty good job of cleaning the cobwebs out of the dark corners of my mind. But being back here with Ryan made it hard to remember we had moved on.

"I need to apologize to you. I've been having a really hard time with the history of your family. I've been fighting with myself over it. I know it's stupid. In my heart I know that."

I swallowed the lump that had formed in my throat. "Thanks."

"That said, I have to tell you, this prom thing is a terrible idea, and I have to wonder what you were thinking when you agreed to it."

"I didn't *agree* to it," I said, unable to hide my annoyance. "I fought against it. I did everything I could to dissuade them, but the committee had already decided to do the vampire-witch thing. At least with me involved, I can do my best to steer things. They were gonna do this with or without me, Ryan."

"I don't like it. It's too close to home."

"I agree, but there's nothing I can do to stop it."

He nodded. "I know we're on the same side, AJ. It's just hard when you factor in our pasts. I don't wanna be doubtful. I'm trying not to be. But that demon really seemed convinced you would betray us and join the snaky side of your family. Like it knows something we don't."

I wanted to be angry with Ryan for asking these questions—for drawing these conclusions. I wanted to scream at him for being unfair and hurtful. But the truth was, he was looking at the situation with an eye that nobody else in the family dared to. Because if we actually dug deeper, we would all see the same parallel. The Serpentines betrayed their allies because of a prophecy that might never have happened. And now they would do anything to make sure it *didn't* happen.

Part of that "anything" seemed to include bringing me back into the fold of the clan.

Ryan was right to question things, not because I had any intention of joining the family, but because if we ignored such an obvious connection, we wouldn't see the whole picture. I took a deep breath and looked into his eyes.

"I understand. I do. And I'm not angry or hurt. I just

hope you know that *this* is my family. You. Rick. The boys. Aunt D. Y'all are my family. Not those stupid power-hungry snakes. Okay?"

He wanted to believe me; I could see it. But his eyes gave him away. No matter how hard he tried, he couldn't hide the doubt that lingered. In that instant, they made another permanent mark on my heart.

"Can we search for the runes together?" I asked. "That way you can keep an eye on me and if I do anything suspicious, you can just smack some sense into me."

He laughed. "Maybe I can get Dad to teach me a proper smacking spell."

I lowered myself out of the tree house, the one place that I had always thought of as ours. Now it was just another casualty of our complicated relationship.

I sat in the tire swing and watched Ryan walk away. It was such an odd feeling, living in the same house but feeling worlds apart. There was no anger, no hatred, but no . . . connection, either. It was like an earthquake had shaken the ground open and now we stood on either side of the crack as it continued to grow wider. I was glad to be over him, but I really missed our bond. It was lonely on this side of the crack.

Where are you? Auntie Tave's voice sounded like a bass

drum in my head. I was not in the mood for her intrusion. Obviously, I couldn't hide my emotions when it came to Ryan, but I had to try.

I took a deep breath and tried to clear my mind, but a very male, very British voice interrupted. *Hello, love, we'll be right round.*

Was I hallucinating? And if so, who the hell did I just dream up? Despite my affinity for all things British (thank you, BBC America), the last thing I needed was someone else in my head.

"A thing for us Brits, eh? Good to know," the guy attached to the voice said as he approached the swing. He was tall, probably six-four, with cropped reddish blond hair, a goatee, and a smile so cocky that I was torn between wanting to slap it off his face and wanting to stare at it for hours.

"I prefer the latter of those two choices, if you don't mind," he said.

"Quit that!" I said, jumping out of the tire swing. "Get out of my head, asshole."

He lifted a pale eyebrow and cocked another smile. "Asshole, is it? No, love, the name is Lex."

"Lex, behave. You're impossible," Tave called as she crossed the yard. Another man was with her, not nearly as hot as Lex. He had a sweet look about him, harmless and kind, with saddish eyes. He reminded me of a turtle.

"Now, that's funny. I can totally see it, too. Hey, Robbie, slow and steady wins the race, mate."

Robbie flipped him the bird, and Lex barked with laughter. "That's a lad. C'mon, Auntie Tave, get over here so I can stop messin' with your girl."

"That was your choice, Alexander."

"Well, I do love having a bit of fun."

"Tave, would you please tell me what the hell is going on?" I said, frustration causing my voice to pitch. "Why can he read my mind? At least you only read my emotions. I don't need this jerk in my head, I don't care who he is."

Lex's laughter spilled over me like a warm shower. Sadly, that warm shower did not clean up the dirty thoughts that traveled through my head. The more I tried to stop them, the more they came. *Dammit. Stop. Don't look at the hot guy. No. Don't think about the hot guy. Dammit. Don't think hot.* Where was this coming from?

My cheeks burned. Lex winked at me, and I noticed his right eye was brown and his left eye was ocean blue. I swallowed hard and concentrated on thinking about marshmallows and baby ducks.

He chuckled then, low and throaty.

Dammit.

"Alexander Archer, get out of her head. Now."

"Yes, ma'am," Lex said, totally without remorse. And then I heard his voice in my head: *You're a tasty bit of yum yourself, love.*

Lex Archer was bad news, and strangely enough, I couldn't seem to wait to read all about it. Two minutes ago I was reminiscing over my lost love, and now I was in heat over some asshole Brit who looked good enough to eat.

I felt another set of eyes on me. I glanced up to Ryan's room and saw him watching from the window.

"Bloke's got it bad, he does," Lex said.

"For me?" I laughed. "He's my stepbrother."

"Hmm, complicated. I like complicated." Lex stepped next to me and held out his hand.

I took his hand and nearly leaped off the ground when the spark jolted from my palm through my body, throwing me slightly off balance.

"Complicated indeed," he said, confirming he'd felt the spark as well. Our gazes met, and for a moment my mind was blank. Totally free of thought or emotion. I may have even stopped breathing for a minute.

"Alexander, let go of her hand. She's not ready for you, and you know it."

"She will be."

Tave gave him the stink-eye and he chuckled again. "I'm sorry, hon. I tried to stop him, but my nephew has a mind of his own," she said. "So you've met Lex. This is his brother, Robbie Archer. And they're going to train you."

"Train me? For what?" I asked.

"Hang on, we need all the kids here." Auntie Tave put her fingers to her lips and whistled. "Ryan, round up the troops. Bring Aunt D, too."

I laughed. "I see Mississippi has rubbed off on you, Auntie Tave. You whistle like you were born here."

Ryan disappeared from the window, and in record time all the kids were standing in the yard with us. Oz, Rayden, and the twins were goofing off with each other, but Ryan stood there as somber as a funeral director.

"Your parents, Doreen, and I had a long talk last night," Aunt Tave began. "It's apparent that none of you are in any position to fight a Bborim. And with AJ struggling to keep the Serpentines out of her head at night, it won't be long before they decide to bring in an empath." She turned to me, grabbed my hand, and squeezed. "If they do that, you're screwed, sweetie."

"Gee, Tave. Don't hold back. Why don't you tell me how you really feel?" I said, smarting from her bluntness.

"What does that have to do with us?" Ryan asked.

"We know the baby is in danger and we all have to work together to protect it. We also know the Serpentines believe that AJ is the key to the runes—which they are desperate to get hold of. They'll use whatever weakness they can against AJ. Including you guys. So I brought my nephews Lex and Robbie here to train her. They're gonna work with y'all a bit, too, but basically, AJ's the main target, so she gets the most training."

"Oh, dude! Are we gonna learn how to do some fancy vampire-ninja moves?" Oz was practically bouncing with excitement.

"Actually, dearie, I'll be trainin' you lads. We've got to up your spell-castin' level. Yer little pranks won't get ye very far with the likes of a Bborim."

"But we'll be workin' with you, too," Robbie said. "You need to learn to keep empaths out of your mind as well. Just remember, some of us are very strong and can read most everyone's minds, and some of us," he looked at Lex, "can only work with one person at a time."

Lex rolled his eyes. "Believe me, one is plenty."

Robbie smiled at me, blushing slightly. Now that Robbie and Lex were standing next to each other, you could tell they were brothers. Actually, they could have been twins, except for a few slight differences. Robbie was an inch or so shorter than his brother and carried himself with less confidence. His eyes, though, were the mirror image of Lex's. His left eye was brown and his right eye blue. His hair was a little more brown than strawberry, and he kept it shaggy, compared to the short crop that Lex wore. Robbie also had a dusting of freckles sprinkled across the bridge of his nose. I gauged both guys to be in their early twenties, but they could easily pass for younger if necessary.

"You gauge right," Lex said. "I'm twenty-one, Robbie here is twenty. But for the next few weeks, we're both eighteen. Going back to school will be fun."

Tave let out an exasperated sigh. "Really, Alexander. You shouldn't do that to her unless you're in training. You should be more respectful than that."

"I'm training her right now, Auntie. If she wants me out of her head, she has to work at it."

Ryan eyed Lex with suspicion before he stepped over to him, held out his hand, and introduced himself. "Ryan Fraser."

Lex and Robbie both shook his hand.

"These are my brothers, Oz and Rayden, and the twins here are my stepsisters Ana and Ainsley."

The girls smiled and giggled a bit. They were going to enjoy this a little too much.

"Wait. Stop. What did you mean, 'school'? Are they training me or following me?" I asked Tave.

"Both. They're going to be training you and protecting you," Auntie Tave said.

"Bodyguards? I have bodyguards?"

A smile slowly spread across Lex's face. "Do you feel special?"

"Hardly. When does this 'training' begin?"

He winked. "No time like the present, love."

Chapter 6

W here are we going to do this? Won't it be a little weird if someone sees you teaching me how to fight demons and vampires?" I asked.

"Dinna fash yeself one bit about that, dearie. C'mon, laddies, yer first lesson is right now." Aunt D led the boys to the center of the yard.

"Ryan, this spell is difficult, but ye need to learn it. Rayden, go fetch my satchel with the herbs. And I need my agrimony extract. Ye'll find it in the spice rack in the kitchen. I was using it just this mornin'."

"What are y'all doing?" Ana asked.

"We'll be casting a protection bubble. To the outside

world the backyard will appear empty, no matter what is actually happening. And with the agrimony, we'll be warding off evil. It's a strong protector. The Bborim won't be able to come into the house or into this yard without permission."

Rayden came back with Aunt D's satchel and a small, dark vial. Aunt D began her ministrations while Ryan watched attentively. There was something strangely sexy about watching him learn.

"So we're gonna train here?" I asked.

"We have plenty of space in the garden, so how about we get started. We can use the trees, the fence, the house, and even the tree house as training grounds," Lex suggested.

My eyes widened at the mention of the tree house, and I shot Lex a look that should have burned the flesh from his bones.

"Or *not* the tree house," he said, holding his hands up.

"Ryan, pay attention! This is important," Aunt Doreen chastised. "One wrong word or motion and, instead of a protection spell, we could have a pontification spell. And then none of ye would ever shut up." I looked to see Ryan watching Lex and me intently.

"Sorry, love. Didn't know it was such a sensitive place.

Robbie, I believe this girl is trainable. She's already keeping things from me."

Robbie had barely uttered a word since his introduction. He just stood there, constantly jotting things down on his clipboard. Finally, he looked up and said, "I think I know how to start. I'll be right back." He took off toward the house.

"He's a weird little bugger," Lex said. "But he's a good guy. Too smart for his own good and desperately needs to get laid, but other than that—"

I snorted as I tried to suppress a giggle but failed miserably. Octavia released a heavy sigh.

"Honestly, Alexander. I'm beginning to wonder if this was such a good idea. I think I'm going to call Delilah at headquarters and ask her to send me a new trainer."

"Headquarters?" Ainsley asked. "What headquarters?"

I was glad she was being nosy, because I was wondering the same thing.

"Headquarters is a lot like Quantico for the FBI, only it's for all these dual-color-eyed miscreants," Tave said with a mock scowl.

"So vampires born with two different-colored eyes are automatically destined to be trainers?" I asked. "Are they all direct Serpentine descendants?"

"Not always. Most are a mix like you," Tave said. "My sister is their mom. We're half Serpentine, but our family is mostly human. When these two were born, both had that clear blue eye and brooding brown, and we knew their destinies. Though I'm seriously doubting whether or not you're the right fit for this job, Alexander."

"Gutted. You've just gutted me," Lex said as he dramatically put his hand over his heart and fell against the tree. "I can't go on now, knowing I've disappointed the greatest auntie in the world."

"You're such a clown. Just tone it down for me, okay? AJ is my goddaughter and she's barely eighteen."

"I'm not a baby, Auntie Tave. Besides, he might be hot and British, which, as he's figured out, are two things I'm really into, but he's also a total dick, so you don't have anything to worry about. He's just not my type."

Lex's voice rang in my head: *I consider that a challenge.*

Be prepared for great disappointment, I thought back.

He laughed as Auntie Tave eyed us both.

"Can I stay and watch?" Oz asked.

"Me too!" Rayden said.

"Us too!" the twins chimed in.

Lex nodded. "All right. But you'll need to be on your

toes. It may get a little rough, and you might have to move quickly or get hurt."

Robbie was heading back our way, carrying a black satchel. Ryan and the kids pulled up some lawn chairs by the driveway to watch.

This was not going to be fun.

"I disagree. I think it will be loads of fun," Lex said.

"You've *got* to stop doing that," I said, brimming with frustration. "I'm not having a conversation with you if I'm just *thinking* something. Stay out of my head."

"Sorry, you've got to make me. That's the point. Either block me or get used to me."

Fucker.

"Potty-minded little thing, aye?" He laughed. "Here comes Robbie now. C'mon, sailor, let's get started."

"Sailor? Oh, because I have a mouth like one. Hah! You should do stand-up."

"I do." *You should try it with me*, he said in my head. Heat scorched my face, and I swallowed. No innuendo there at all.

"Dream on," I responded.

"You don't have to worry about that one, sailor. I will."

"If you two are through with this foreplay, I'd like to

start working with AJ. I'll let you know when she's ready, Lex, then you can begin to pound each other into dust," Robbie said, making me jump. I had completely forgotten he had joined us.

Lex smiled, and my belly flipped.

This was going to be very messy.

"You can teach me to block him from my thoughts?" I asked Robbie as Lex walked over to talk to Tave.

"I can. But it won't be easy. He's good. And he likes you, which is bad. The more you interest him, the more determined he'll be to stay in your head."

"I'm a fast learner. Get him out."

"Okay, but in order for you to learn, you'll have to take these. They're basically an empath inhibitor. They'll help you while you physically train, but it won't do all the work for you. You'll have to learn to block him while you fight. I'll work with you during your downtime."

Robbie handed me a couple of grass-green horse pills. I eyed them suspiciously. There was no way I could swallow these things without something to drink. To my surprise, he pulled a bottle of water from his bag and handed it to me.

"You'll take these pills before each training session until I think you're strong enough to go at it drug-free. I'll be working with you and your sisters on fine-tuning your other extrasensory skills, like hearing, night vision, smell. Ana and Ainsley seem to function on their own frequency, and I haven't been able to find it. If I can't find it, then chances are others won't be able to, either," Robbie said.

"I can feel Lex in my head, but you're like a stealth bomber."

"Most people don't feel me. Lex doesn't have the mental discipline to do stealth."

I grinned, then choked down the pills. "Now what?" I asked.

"Have you been taught how to focus?" Robbie asked.

"Yes. And Auntie Tave has been trying to teach me to take it deeper, but either I'm a difficult student or she's a terrible teacher, because we haven't gotten very far."

"It's not easy to trick a part of your brain into shutting down. At first, closing the door to your thoughts will be temporary. You'll have to work on it every day and you'll have to do it while being active. Fighting, running, doing schoolwork. You'll get headaches and you'll be angry and frustrated, but you have to keep working at it. The pills will help, but Lex will be ruthless. He'll use your thoughts against you, do whatever he can to weaken you, and will laugh when he bests you.

You've got a lot of work to do if you really want him out of your head."

"Just tell me what to do."

C'mon, sailor, ye can do better than that.

His taunts were incessant. Every time I blocked him he'd fly at me, and as soon as I dodged his assault, the door to my brain would open right up.

You've got to do better. The Bborim will eat you for lunch.

I jumped to the top of the tire swing, held on to the rope, and swung myself back and forth. Robbie said the best way to learn was to make sure I was doing something active while trying to block the empath. I had to learn to make my brain ambidextrous.

"C'mon, AJ! Kick his ass!" Oz yelled.

"Roscoe, I'll scrub that tongue with bitters if I hear that again," Aunt D scolded.

Ryan stood at the side of the house as rigid as a broomstick, watching.

Sweat trickled down my neck. For at least an hour we had been sparring with each other while Lex silently taunted me. I felt him inside my head, but when I pushed to get him out, he'd push right back in.

"Let's go, children. Leave yer sister to her trainin',"

Aunt D said, forcing my audience to leave. I sighed in relief when Ryan walked away with them.

Now maybe I could focus.

I concentrated and rocked the tire swing higher and higher. Finally, a noticeable silence filled my head. I took advantage of the peace and leaped from the tire to a tree branch, grabbing with both hands and dismounting like a gymnast going for the gold.

Surprise lit up Lex's face as I flipped midair and landed on top of him, taking him to the ground, flat on his back.

His pupils dilated and his breathing became raspy.

I inhaled, taking in his scent, and adrenaline surged through me. My fangs popped out and I began to salivate like a wolf over a fresh kill.

His pulse kicked up a notch, and suddenly I was ravenous.

I licked my lips when I saw a heartbeat thrumming in his neck. The temptation to bite him and feel the warm blood trickle over my tongue kicked my own pulse up a notch.

I lowered my head to his neck and slowly licked his pulse. He moaned, grabbed my wrists, and flipped me to the ground.

My control began to slip. I hissed and fought him, but he was much stronger and much more restrained than me. "Easy. Easy now," he said in a soothing voice. "I know, love. The adrenaline does that to all of us from time to time." I wriggled and writhed beneath him as anger and confusion collided inside me. "There, now. C'mon. Close your eyes and take a deep breath. Focus, sailor. You can do it."

As soon as he called me "sailor," laughter tumbled out of me, until I was gasping for breath and tears were trailing down my face. It was an instant release, like nothing I had felt before.

Lex released my wrists and I slid out from under him, sitting up against the tree. The last of the giggling fit finally began to ebb. Lex scooted next to me. Smiling, he wiped the tears from my cheeks.

"You did good tonight," he said.

"I could do better," I answered.

"Yes, and you will." He said it like there was no question. I *would* do better.

"Um, sorry about the almost-biting-you thing." My cheeks burned when I spoke.

He cocked a brow and smirked. "I was tempted to let you try. Have you never bitten before?" he asked.

"Do you know how to feed without killing or creating a dichamp?"

"What?" My face must have betrayed my horror.

Lex chuckled. "So, that's no, then? Another lesson for you, it seems. Every vampire needs to learn how to feed. There's no guarantee we'll always have hemoshakes available. What would you do then?"

I had no idea.

"Feeding for nourishment is not brutal. You can feed off animals and leave them alive and well when you're finished. For flavor, I recommend cattle. For the hunt, I recommend grizzly bears. Ferocious buggers."

"How will you teach me?" I asked.

He held up his wrist. "I'll be your guinea pig, sailor. And if you're in the mood for a hunt, I can be a grizzly bear, too."

Was he kidding?

Chapter 7

I watched as the pulse at his wrist drummed slowly, like he had no concerns whatsoever. Like if I bit into him, everything would be just fine.

Like there was no possibility of me killing him, or changing him into a dichamp. Like I was a pro at this sort of thing.

"You're out of your mind," I said, throwing his wrist back at him. "I can't just feed off you. That's crazy."

"You can. And you need to. Just remember, you don't have to inject the venom when you bite. It won't happen if you don't want it to."

Yeah, right.

His blue eye glittered in the moonlight as his dark

eye blended into the night. "I know you can do this—just concentrate."

"What if I break my concentration and accidentally inject you?"

"Then Robbie will fix me right up with one of his fancy potions. Plus, I'm a trainer. We're built differently. We're made of sturdy stock. Trust me."

His voice touched me like an evening breeze as he held his wrist up to me again.

My hands were shaky as I took his forearm and inhaled deeply. His scent was an intoxicating mix of sweat, dirt, and clover. My fangs descended immediately.

I was in total control, but I was completely compelled to taste him. I had never wanted something so much before in my life. And besides, what vampire didn't know how to feed? Seriously. I would be a disgrace to my species if I didn't give it a try.

His pulse skipped a beat, but other than that, it continued at a slow and steady pace. Robbie had been wrong, Lex had plenty of mental discipline. I lifted his wrist to my mouth and licked along the blue vein that tempted me. If I was going to bite him, the least I could do was numb the area first.

"It won't hurt. You don't have to lick me first."

I wanted to, I thought, allowing him to hear me.

His pulse jumped again but went immediately back to the steady *thum-thump, thum-thump, thum-thump* that my own heart began to mimic.

His scent and taste filled my senses as I lowered my fangs to his flesh. The skin resisted at first, but I pressed forward until it gave way with a tiny sigh, and the tangy smell of blood suddenly overwhelmed me.

My heart raced to warp speed. "Easy, there. Concentrate. Suck slowly and concentrate. Keep your venom at bay." Lex's voice was a harsh whisper, like he was in pain.

Am I hurting you? I asked silently as I slowly began to drink from him. The warm, metallic liquid was better than any hemoshake I'd ever tasted.

Not like you mean, he answered. *Just a few more sips— don't drain me, love.*

I wanted to keep feeding. The rush that washed through me was better than any adrenaline high. I sucked harder, swallowing loudly, unable to stop feeding. My mind tried to tell my mouth what to do, but apparently my mouth wasn't listening.

Lex groaned quietly, then whispered in my mind, *I need you to stop or I won't be able to.*

Just one more drink. That's all I wanted. I drew in one last drop, letting the flavors burst over my tongue. I licked his arm clean and forced myself to let go.

The broken flesh on Lex's arm began to seal immediately. I had never seen a blood-weakened vampire heal so quickly.

I felt a trickle of blood trail from my mouth, and I flicked my tongue out to catch it. My eyes rolled to the back of my head as I enjoyed the last taste.

"I'm sorry," Lex said. "I thought I was strong enough, but I'm not."

"Did I drink too much? Shit, I knew this was a bad idea. I'll go get you a hemoshake right now," I said in a panic.

"No, sailor, that's not it. I'm sorry for this." Lex reached out and pulled me to him. He held my face a breath away from his and inhaled. "You smell complicated," he said just as his lips touched mine.

I might smell complicated, but he tasted dangerous. And apparently, I was really fond of that flavor.

Lex's lips sighed over mine, and I fell into him like he was a down comforter. There was nothing unsure or shy about the way he wrapped me up, laid me down, and took control.

My entire body lit up like a flare. He was strong and sure and so damn sexy that I completely lost myself to the kiss.

I never knew lips could be soft and firm at the same time. He didn't rush it, but still my pulse sailed into orbit. Lex's tongue touched mine and I hungrily responded.

Easy, he said in my head. *The slower the better.*

I breathed him in and allowed myself to indulge in the feel of him. He moved from my mouth to my neck, nibbling up to my ear. A strange noise escaped from my throat.

This was so different. So new. And it was scary as hell. I had never felt such an instant attraction to someone I didn't even know.

He must have read my thoughts, because he pulled back immediately. "I'm truly sorry. No excuse for what I just did. I've never done that before."

"Well, that's a lie," I said with a nervous laugh.

Lex chuckled. "I mean, I've never lost control with someone I was training before. You've a bit of an effect on me, it seems."

I sat back against the tree and really took him in. He had taken his shirt off during our training session. He was lean and muscular. Very defined. There was a tattoo on his left arm that covered almost the entire area between his shoulder and elbow. It was a wooden stake, wrapped in the Serpentine "S" piercing a heart.

I reached out and traced the "S" part of the design. "Is this your birthmark?" I asked. Even half-bloods like us got the family mark.

He nodded, drawing his eyebrows together.

"What is it?"

Lex looked up at Ryan's window. "Your lad's been watching, and he's none too happy. He doesn't trust me."

Suddenly I felt Ryan's eyes on me. After all those times watching him with Lindsey, I knew exactly what he felt right now. No matter how much you thought you were over someone, it was never easy to see them with someone new.

Chapter 8

obbie gave me two more horse pills to take before bed, and I slept like the dead. Or would that be the undead? I couldn't remember the last time I had a dreamless sleep, but this morning I woke rested and full of energy.

I also woke up sore as hell. My body ached in places that I didn't even know had muscles. I took an extra-long hot shower, hoping to work out the stiffness in my shoulders and legs. And butt. And back. And sides.

I was one big ouch right now. I even had to sit on the bed to put on my jeans because I couldn't manage the pain while standing up. I felt like Grandma Moses.

Someone knocked on my door as I was grabbing my

backpack. I opened it to find Ryan hovering in the doorway like a dark storm cloud. His eyes were hard, his mouth grim, his jaw clenched.

"I don't trust him," he said, pushing his way through and closing the door behind him.

"C'mon in," I said, rolling my eyes.

"I'm not gonna waste time. I don't like that guy, I don't trust him, and if you want to keep the family safe, I think you need to stay away from him. He's dangerous."

My mind flashed to last night and Lex offering me his wrist to feed from. Then to Lex laying me on the moss and kissing me until I was wet-noodle limp. Yeah, he was definitely dangerous.

"You're just jealous. And you have no right to be, Ryan. You've got a girlfriend. You've moved on. It's my turn."

"This isn't about that. I care about protecting you and the baby. And that vampire is a threat to our security. I don't care whose nephew he is. So move on, just not with him."

The way Ryan spat the word "vampire" made my mouth sour. Like saying the word made him physically ill.

"That *vampire* is training me to use my abilities. Teaching me how to block the bad guys from my thoughts. You don't get to tell me who is dangerous until you've had one of those evil bastards invading your thoughts and your dreams on a regular basis. Trust me when I tell you Lex is far from bad. Dangerous? Maybe. But not in the way you're implying."

Ryan's face reddened as he processed my words. I pushed past him, not wanting to hear anything else he might have to say. But he grabbed my arm and pulled me back.

"You don't mean that," he said, his eyes finally softening. I wanted to be like the boy in *Charlie and the Chocolate Factory* and dive right into those dark-chocolate pools and let them carry me away.

But I couldn't. I wouldn't.

Sadness filled me when I realized that I had been holding back, holding out hope. I had been standing in my own way when it came to getting over Ryan. But not anymore.

"I'm sorry, Ryan. But I really do mean it. You were the only person I had ever felt truly connected with, until Lex. Something's there, and I need to explore it. And you have no say in what I do. None."

His eyes hardened. "I have no say in what you do, but I have every right to protect my family. I don't trust him."

"I do."

"You trusted Mr. Charles, too, and look where that got you," Ryan said as he walked out the door.

Ouch. Score one for Ryan Fraser.

I headed downstairs and entered a tension-filled kitchen. A clean-shaven and almost baby-faced Lex was already there, flirting with Aunt D and making her giggle like a schoolgirl. Robbie sat quietly at the table, thumbing through a textbook and scribbling notes. And Ryan just sat there quietly fuming.

"Hello, sailor," Lex said with a wink as I walked in. "Everything all right?" *Should I have a little chat with duffer?*

Not necessary. "Everything's great. You guys ready for your first day of school?" I said, faking cheeriness.

"Oz! Rayden! Are y'all coming with me or not?" Ryan bellowed. "The bus is leaving, so get on board or get to walking."

Rayden and Oz clambered down the stairs and out the door. Ryan shot a look at me, then slammed the door as he walked out.

"Duffer needs to work on his poker face," Lex said.

"Aye," Aunt D agreed. "He wears his heart on his sleeve, he does. Just like his da did at that age."

"Are the twins still here?" I asked. Usually they were

chomping at the bit to get out the door. The earlier they got to school, the better their social life.

"No, they caught a ride with a friend. Been gone a while."

"Okay, then I guess it's our turn. Let's do this thing," I said to Robbie and Lex.

Lex placed his palm on my lower back, sending a jolt of friction through my system. The hairs on my neck stood at full alert, and my heart tumbled for the umpteenth time since I'd met him.

Did he feel that, too? I glanced up at his smooth face to see a slow smile spreading, creating deep dimples on both cheeks. *You're not the only one.*

"You've got to get out of my head," I said as Lex opened the driver's-side door for me.

"You've got to make me. Robbie and I will follow you. See you at school, sailor."

I flipped him off and started the car.

He laughed. "You never fail to disappoint."

The buzz about the hot new British guys made the rounds fast, so I was very popular by second period. A group of girls was waiting for me at my locker between classes.

"Who are they?"

"Where did they come from?"

"Do they need escorts?"

"How do you know them?"

I exchanged my books, rolling my eyes while they bombarded me with questions. When the hum and chatter died down, I finally said, "Lex is the taller one, Robbie is the quiet one. They're my godmother's nephews. They'll be here for the rest of the semester. They don't bite, so if you have any other questions, ask them."

I pushed through the crowd to where Malia and Bridget were waiting to bombard me with the exact same questions. Bridget opened her mouth and I held up my hand. "Stop," I said before she could speak. "I'm on my way to meet them. Walk with me and see for yourself."

This was probably the worst idea I'd ever had. Well, if I really wanted Lex to, you know, continue noticing me, that is. Bridget with her auburn curls, freckled nose, sweet smile, and curves that should come with a DAN-GER sign attached. Then there was Malia with her exotic looks—darker skin, beautiful eyes, sleek black hair, and, again, curves that should come with a warning. I looked like a lanky, pale, blond dust mop compared to the two of them.

We reached the main office, where Lex and Robbie

were finishing up their registration and getting their schedules. Lex was busy charming the office secretary, but when we arrived, he looked up and caught my gaze. *Not even close to a dust mop.*

I stopped short and swallowed. He had to stop doing that.

"You okay?" Bridget asked.

"Fine. Just, um—" I couldn't break away from Lex's stare.

"Just some major eye candy," Malia finished for me. "Wow. No wonder you're tongue-tied."

Lex strolled out of the office, with Robbie following behind. I introduced them to my friends and was bowled over to see Malia smile and bat her eyes when she shook Robbie's hand. Robbie's eyes went wide, and his cheeks turned deep scarlet. For a brief moment, his poker face was gone. He was smitten. And by the look on Malia's face, the feeling was mutual.

Very. Bad. Idea, I thought.

Agreed, Lex chimed in.

I shot him a look and he gave me a cheeky grin. *Work for it, sailor.*

"Let me see your schedule," I said. "I'll tell you where you're going next."

I glanced at the printout. "Looks like we have several classes together. Starting now. Let's get a move on before we're late. Being tardy in Crabby Crandall's class isn't the best idea—especially on your first day."

As soon as we walked into Crandall's classroom, I felt assaulted by the tension radiating from Ryan. He sat at his desk scowling straight ahead, his arms folded across his chest and anger bubbling out of every pore.

The bell rang as I took my seat. Robbie and Lex handed Crabby Crandall their schedules. She eyed them suspiciously, then said, "You barely made it to your seat in time, Miss Ashe. One more tardy this semester and it's detention for you. Boys, take a seat. Class, this is Alexander and Robert Archer."

The girls let out a collective sigh. Seriously, it was no wonder Lex had an ego the size of a large continent. Sure, there was some advantage to knowing every girl's thoughts, but how boring would that be? No challenge.

I do like a challenge. Lex's voice echoed in my head.

I glanced over my shoulder and cocked a brow.

He slowly grinned.

And just to be clear, I think you might be the biggest challenge I've ever had.

Chapter 9

The rest of the day seemed to fly by. I was almost surprised when the bell rang and school was over.

Lex and Robbie were waiting for me at my locker. "Ready to train?" Lex asked.

"Not yet. I've got prom committee now. We have a lot to do and no time to do it."

"Prom? Oh, this should be fun. I think I'll tag along. You comin', mate?" he asked Robbie.

"It's all you," Robbie answered. "I think I can find somethin' else to entertain me for a while."

I followed his gaze to the end of the hall, where Malia stood. She was biting her lip and smiling in Robbie's direction.

"Rob, not the best idea. She's human. You can't risk it," Lex warned.

"Says the chap who has played with every human who's tickled his fancy. There's somethin' about her, mate. Let me have this."

"We'll talk about it tonight. Just don't be stupid."

"Yeah, yeah," Robbie said absentmindedly as he walked toward Malia.

"This is not good," I said.

"Not good at all," Lex agreed. "We'll sort it out tonight. Now let's go plan a prom."

The committee was meeting with Mrs. Christopher to discuss historical details we could include in the decorations. She had been so excited when we told her the plans and the theme. I was still a little nervous about it hitting so close to home, but I was also secretly starting to get excited about the idea of being "out" for one night. Living life in the vampire closet wasn't fun.

We were almost to Mrs. Christopher's classroom when Lex stopped and put his finger to his mouth, warning me to be quiet.

Listen.

I focused and opened my hearing. Ryan was in the room with Mrs. Christopher, asking her some questions.

Very specific questions.

"Mrs. Christopher, you said something in class the other day about artifacts at the library. What kind of artifacts?"

"They're on display in the lobby as well as in the Valley Springs archive room. Some pretty amazing pieces, actually. There's a mortar and pestle that's in mint condition. Really special."

"Where were these artifacts found?" he asked.

"Well, many of them were passed down from my own ancestors. I will often loan out or rotate some of my family pieces for display. Other pieces were excavated just outside of town—where the historical marker and that old church are located?"

He's starting the rune search. Smart lad to start with her. Now that I'm here, he'll never work with you.

I shook my head and opened up my senses. I had been working with Robbie on reading the moods of others. I took a deep breath and concentrated. I didn't believe Ryan was going behind my back. Maybe I could read his mood and know for sure.

But as soon as I closed my eyes, a distant buzzing began to hum in my head.

We're here. Listening. Watching. Join us. Embrace your destiny.

It was exactly what had happened in the fall when I

touched the Serpentine Scrolls, but this time I didn't need to touch a piece of charmed parchment to be pulled into another place.

My body felt heavy, like it was full of sand, and my skin tingled as it hummed.

One minute I was in the hallway at school, and the next I was surrounded by a crowd of chanting, hooded figures on a beach. The night air was damp and dark, and I could taste the salt from the ocean. The man with the ice-blue eyes stood next to me. He was holding out his hand to me, encouraging me to take it and join him. Just like he had done almost every night since the first moment I had touched the scrolls.

My mind was pulling away, but my hand was acting on its own, reaching out to him.

The chanting grew louder.

Something told me this wasn't a parallel universe like I had always believed. And it wasn't a dream, either. Wherever it was, it was happening in real time. And if I accepted his hand, somehow I would no longer be able to return to the halls of Valley Springs High School.

As much as I loved the ocean, this was not my idea of a five-star vacation.

Hooded Evil's fingertips touched mine and I jumped.

If you take my hand, we won't harm your mother.

In my heart I knew he wasn't trustworthy, but I couldn't seem to stop myself from reaching out to him.

You're stronger than they are, sailor. Fight him. Fight them. Don't let them win.

Lex's voice was a lighthouse to my lost dinghy. I zeroed in on the sound. *Please keep talking.*

Come back to me or you'll be late for prom committee. I'm not prepared to face those girls all alone. I need you to protect me.

There was a lot to be said for a man who could make me laugh while I was being wooed to the dark side by Hooded Evil.

I searched my mind for Lex and then I saw him. He was on the beach with me but standing outside the circle of doom. The lighthouse analogy really worked, as he was the only bright spot in the darkness.

Hooded Evil's ice-blue eyes widened as I pulled away, walked through the crowd, and let Lex guide me to safety.

I squinted under the harsh fluorescent lights of the hallway. Lex's warm hand held mine and I felt safe.

"Thank you," I whispered as I stood on my tiptoes and kissed him softly.

He smiled beneath my lips and said, "After that kiss, I should be thanking you."

Prom committee was painful. Everyone, including Mrs. Christopher, fawned over Lex: He spread his charm thick, like soft butter on a warm roll. But by the end of the meeting, we all had agreed that "Love Sucks" would be the theme and that dressing up as vampires or witches would be highly encouraged. Mrs. Christopher even generously offered the use of an old family tiara to crown this year's queen.

But now we were back at the house under the protection of Aunt D's magic bubble, where Lex was promptly kicking my ass—and enjoying it just a little too much.

You'd better work harder for it, sailor. Hooded Evil will come at you like a wolverine. We'll do this all night if we have to.

I was flat on my back, with Lex straddling me. He had my wrists pinned above my head and a very dangerous look on his face.

Robbie had told me the reason Lex was so good at his job was that he was ruthless when it came to using the person's weaknesses against them. I decided to do the same.

I smiled.

All night? Maybe I'll just take you up on that.

Lex smirked. I found the inner strength to wipe my mind clean as I leaned forward off the ground. His grip on my wrists loosened enough that I managed to slip my left arm out. I put my hand on his cheek, slowly licked my lips, and pulled his mouth to mine.

Just as he breathed into me, I pulled my other arm free and, with the force of a wrestler on steroids, threw him off me. He flew backward, hitting the side of the house with a crash.

I jumped into the air and really tried to maintain a steady hover while I also worked at keeping Lex out of my head. It was hard, especially since I was so bad at the floating midair thing. Why the hell I hadn't tuned in to my super skills earlier is beyond me.

Sweat poured out of me.

It took about a half a beat for Lex to recover. I couldn't read his face, and because I still had him blocked, I had no idea what he was thinking.

Suddenly he flew at me like a bullet, and I lost my concentration and fell about fifteen feet. But intentional or not, this ended up being a wise move, because he flew over me, landing on a tree branch.

I flew to a branch just above him. I could feel the steady pressure of Lex pushing to get inside my head, so I pushed back. It was like trying to wish away a sinus headache. I had to keep moving, doing, flying, thinking, and working while I blocked him. Robbie said it should become second nature, like breathing.

It was hard to imagine this ever being like second nature. Because even with the aid of the horse pills, no matter how hard I tried to keep the door shut, Lex always found a way in.

Proud of ya, sailor. Got me good with that one. Next time, it won't be so easy to push me away.

I mentally forced him out of my head.

"What makes you think there'll be a next time?" I asked.

I grabbed the limb above me, swung my legs out, and kicked him off the branch. He landed on his feet, just like a cat.

"Nice landing, kitten," I said.

His laugh came from low in his throat, and my belly flipped. I pushed my attraction for him into a dark corner of my mind, kept pushing him out of my thoughts, and dove for him.

Lex stood his ground, so the impact was a bit like

hitting granite, but I managed to make him stumble backward a couple of steps, putting him in a defensive posture.

He worked on my mind, never relenting with his attempt to find a weak spot and push through. But I held strong while we duked it out like the vampire ninjas Oz talked about.

The fighting seemed to come naturally. I never had to think about my next move. However, I had a really hard time analyzing the situation and predicting *his* next move. It took so much effort to keep him out of my head and anticipate his actions.

And he could tell I was struggling, so it was no surprise when he swooped my legs out from underneath me and pinned me to the ground again.

"Told you there'd be a next time." He leaned in, touched his lips softly to mine, then rolled off me.

I sat up and worked to catch my breath. As I leaned back against the tree, my head began to buzz like a swarm of hornets, and goose bumps tore across my skin. "They're trying to get to me again," I said. "Right now." This time I wouldn't give in to them.

"I can't feel them or hear them. Are you sure?"

"Yes, my skin crawls and my head hums when they

start digging around in my thoughts. Last year they did it through me touching the Serpentine Scrolls. Then they were quiet for a while, probably just waiting for me to let my defenses down. But now, for some reason they seem to have a direct line to my noggin."

"I need to talk to Robbie and find out what's up. This shouldn't be happening. Especially within the protection bubble."

"Okay. And while you do that, I'm going to talk to Ryan. I need to make sure we're still on the same page."

"And if you're not?"

I took a deep breath. I really didn't want to believe there was a chance that Ryan didn't trust me. "I guess we'll go with Plan Lex then, whatever you decide that may be."

Chapter 10

I stood outside Ryan's door for what seemed like forever. I dreaded this conversation more than I dreaded second period with Crabby Crandall every day.

Lex said Ryan didn't trust him, but he didn't say why. If it was just jealousy, then we could work through that. At least I hoped we could.

With my heart pounding, I knocked on Ryan's door. He opened it almost immediately.

"I was wondering how long you were going to stand out here," he said. "C'mon in."

His room smelled like him, and a rush of memories flooded over me and had me longing for last summer.

"What's up?" he asked. "I'm getting ready to head out, so can you make this quick?"

"Um, well, a couple of things," I said, pulling at my hair nervously. Why was I so anxious? "First, we need to make a plan to search for the runes. I have some ideas, and I thought maybe we could go out tonight after supper?"

"Sure," he said with a shrug. "Sounds good to me. We need to get going on that if we're going to find them and keep them hidden. I definitely think we need to get them into the house where they'll be safe. Since evil has to be invited in, the runes should be well protected."

"Which is also why we have to make sure Mom doesn't leave the house—she's safe here. So you're still planning to work with me on this?"

His eyes widened. "Of course I am. Why wouldn't I be?" he asked. "Look, I'm having a hard time dealing with your sidekick, I'll admit that, but AJ, I can't imagine you would ever do anything to hurt your family." He paused, then amended, "*Our* family."

I knew in my heart Ryan wasn't going to cut me out. We meant too much to each other, and ultimately we shared the same goal—the safety of our family.

"I'm so relieved. I was worried that maybe you were letting some old feelings for me cloud your judgment of Lex."

"I'll admit it's not easy seeing you with another guy. But then I realized I had no right to be jealous—now I know how you felt seeing Lindsey and me together, and I'm really sorry about that. I don't like seeing you with Lex, but I'm sure that will eventually get easier. You deserve to be happy. I hope he makes you happy."

Conflicting emotions warred inside me. This had been what I'd wanted, right? For Ryan to trust me, for us to keep working together, and for our relationship to truly shift into that of siblings as opposed to star-crossed teenage lovers. So why did it hurt so much to hear him tell me he hoped Lex made me happy?

"Is that all?" Ryan asked.

"Oh, um, no." I mentally shook the cobwebs loose and swept them under a rug. "There's one more thing."

"What's that?"

"The Serpentines got into my head today and managed to pull me into their world, like they did when I touched the scrolls."

He couldn't mask the worry that glittered his eyes. "What happened? Where were you?"

"Actually, I was at school the first time, and at home the second."

"Twice! And here? How did they get through the bubble?"

"I don't know. Lex and Robbie were going to talk to Aunt D about it."

"So what exactly happened? Did they just talk to you?" Ryan asked.

"They tried to keep me with them. The only thing that saved me from staying there permanently was Lex. He went after me and pulled me back."

"Huh," Ryan said absently. "And you didn't touch anything? You were just doing your own thing and suddenly you were yanked there?"

"Pretty much. The first time, Lex and I were walking in the halls at school, and the second time, we were resting after our training session."

"Oh. Okay. Well, thank God you're okay. I think I'm going to run down and talk to Aunt D and see what we can do to strengthen the protection spell. I wouldn't forgive myself if they could get to you because I did something wrong when casting the spell."

I went into my room, picked up my cell phone, and called Bridget.

"Hey," she answered on the second ring. "What's up?"

"I dunno. I feel weird. Ryan just gave me permission to be with Lex, and I'm totally confused."

"Mmm. You and Sexy Lexy? Gotta love that."

"I guess," I answered. "But something isn't right, and I don't know what it is."

"Just go with it, AJ. You're overthinking. If you're still pining for Ryan, even a little bit, well, that's honestly kinda ridiculous. He and Lindsey have been together all year, and even if they weren't, you know you can't be with Ryan. He's your brother now. You've said that so much, I swear it's tattooed on the back of your eyelids. So stop worrying about Ryan and enjoy your time with Sexy Lexy. He seems to be the perfect rebound guy."

"So this is you giving me some tough love, then?" I asked with a laugh.

"Somebody needs to." I could hear her smiling through the phone. "Hey, I hate to cut this short, but I gotta go. You okay now?"

"Yeah. I'm better. Thanks. See ya tomorrow."

I clicked my phone shut as my bedroom door opened. "We've got to go," Lex said.

"Excuse me, but did you forget how to knock?"

"C'mon, we don't have much time. Ryan lied. He's going to look for the runes now, and we have to beat him to it. Now, let's go."

He grabbed my wrist and damn near dragged me

down the stairs. "Let go!" I said. "You're hurting me."

He chuckled and released my wrist. "Sailor, you just kicked my ass a few minutes ago—so that little tug on your wrist didn't hurt you. But nice try."

"Whatever. I can walk without assistance. But you need to tell me what you're talking about."

Robbie was waiting for us in the kitchen. "You haven't told her?" he asked Lex.

"I told her Ryan was lying."

Robbie rolled his eyes. "She might need a bit more of an explanation. Especially now that she thinks you're the one lying to her."

I shot Robbie a look, then glanced over at Lex.

"You're doin' good keeping me out of your head, sailor. But you have to work harder to keep Robbie out. He's the brain ninja, you know."

"Shhh. Let's talk about this outside. I don't want Momma to overhear anything," I said. I knew we were keeping her in the loop, but I wasn't sure she needed to know every detail.

"You don't have to worry about that. She went to the hospital for a checkup."

"What do you mean she *went* to the hospital? Her checkups were supposed to be at home from now on."

I grabbed my cell phone out of my pocket and dialed Auntie Tave.

"Hello there," she answered. "It's been so strange not being able to feel you these past couple of days. I guess training is going well?"

"Tave, are you with Mom? She left the house to go to the hospital for a checkup," I said, ignoring her question.

"Oh no. What was she thinking? Don't worry, I'll find her and get her home safely."

Shit.

Shit. Shit. Shit.

"We've got to go, sailor."

"I can't go anywhere until I know my mom is safe," I said.

My phone rang again.

"She's fine," Auntie Tave said when I answered. "I've called Rick and he's coming to get her. She said she just had to come to the hospital."

"We need to up the protection, Tave. The Serpentines were able to get into my head twice today, and once was here at the house."

"Oh, that's not good. I'm calling Doreen. We'll fix this."

"Make sure Rick casts a protection spell on the car

before he brings Mom home."

Worry sat like a rock in my belly. Momma's condition was already precarious—and this added mind-control thing was a worry we didn't need. What good was living with a family of witches if they couldn't cast a proper protective spell?

I ended the call, looked up, and started when I saw Lex and Robbie watching me intently. I had forgotten they were even there.

"She's safe, then?" Lex asked.

I nodded.

"Good. Then we've got to go."

Chapter 11

ex drove while Robbie explained.

"Ryan lied to you. He and his brothers are on their way to look for the runes."

I started laughing. "Why would he take the kids with him? Don't get me wrong; he loves his brothers, but no way would he take them to look for the runes."

"He's traveling in a group, just like you were told to do. They're headed to the library. Mrs. Christopher gave him some information today that he's going to research."

"This just doesn't make any sense," I said.

"For what it's worth, Ryan had every intention of hunting for the runes with you tonight, until . . ." Robbie paused.

"Until what?"

"Until you told him about your visits from the Serpentines, love," Lex said.

The lightbulb finally burned bright above my head. "You've been with me both times. He thinks you're their connection to me. Wow."

Lex nodded.

"Why didn't you tell me he thought that?" I asked.

"Would you have believed me if I had?" Lex asked.

No. I wouldn't have.

"Ryan's floundering right now. You were his best friend, and now with all the family stress, plus the added pressure of you and Lex, he just doesn't have anyone to trust. He and Bridget have been talking about that a lot lately. They both miss you."

"Why would Bridget miss me? I'm with her all the time."

"Yeah, but she feels a little on the outs because of Malia," Robbie said. "And that Malia—wow, she's something. I can't read her, not even one emotion. Do you know how nice that is?"

I shot Robbie a look as he wandered off topic. "I don't know what's up with Bridget and Malia—they just can't get into a groove. But Ryan has Lindsey. And he has his best friend, Sean," I muttered.

"Love, when was the last time you saw his mate around the house? Or his girl, for that matter?" Lex asked.

I had to think about it. Sean actually hadn't been around since the beginning of the school year. I'd been so wrapped up in my own problems that I hadn't even noticed. And Lindsey? Well, I really couldn't say. "It's been a while for both, I guess."

"Sean and Lindsey are an item now. Ryan's been on his own for weeks."

"But . . . ?" I wanted to argue, but I couldn't. I had been so caught up in trying to get over Ryan, I hadn't even noticed he was all alone.

Robbie leaned forward from the backseat and touched my shoulders. "It's hard, getting information about your friends this way. I know. And it's not fair that we can hear almost everyone's thoughts. Trust me when I say sometimes I wish I couldn't. But we have to tell you this so you'll understand. Ryan is in a bad way right now. And since he feels that Lex is betraying you and therefore betraying your family, he's looking for answers and friendship elsewhere. He's not going to trust you to help him."

I stared out the window as we drove past Bumpers, then town hall, and then the park. I swallowed the lump that had formed in my throat. I was a selfish cow. How could I have been so wrapped up in myself that I didn't even notice what was going on in Ryan's life? The boy I had supposedly loved. And then there was Bridget, my best friend, who wasn't confiding in me at all. Which was ironic, since I had tried to confide in her about my fang-tacular split personality last fall and she had laughed so hard my pride still hurt thinking about it.

"Hey, where are we going?" I asked, realizing we'd bypassed the library for Bridget's neighborhood.

Sure enough, right in front of Bridget's house sat Ryan's Jeep.

"I don't know if I understand why we need to get the runes before he does. Where's the logic in that?" I asked. "Won't that just push him further away?"

Lex shot Robbie a look in the rearview mirror that sent my Spidey sense into orbit.

"What aren't you telling me?" I demanded. "If you expect me to help with this, you have to tell me every-thing."

Lex parked behind Ryan's Jeep, reached over, and took my hand in his. "He's planning to destroy the runes when he finds them. His thoughts are well intended, but there's a slight problem with his plan. He can destroy the runes, but he cannot destroy the magic—not at his skill level. And once the magic is released, we can't control where it will land or what it will do."

I guess this could be a case of the road to a paranormal apocalypse being paved with good intentions?

We sat outside Bridget's house for a few minutes while Robbie and Lex did their brain voodoo.

I really hated the idea that they had no reservations about just getting inside someone's head and listening to their private thoughts. I felt violated every time my dreams were invaded by the Serpentines, every time they whisked me off to some faraway world, but at least I was aware of their infiltration. How awful would it be to have all your private thoughts unknowingly accessed and used against you?

"It's no fun being on the other end, either," Lex said. "Do you know how hard it is, knowing everyone's secrets? Everyone's thoughts about you? About your family? Do you know how difficult it is to even date someone? It's impossible. You're the first girl who has at least been able to push me out of your head. Very few people have a natural ability to block. Your friend Malia is one of them, which is why Robbie can't seem to get her out of his mind."

Robbie's ears turned bright red. "Yeah," he said, nodding. "It's rare to find a girl you know nothing about. Challenging. Intriguing. And wonderfully silent."

I hadn't really thought about that. How noisy their heads must be, and what an awful burden it was to carry all those secrets around. "I'm sorry. I know it must be hard."

"You get used to it, and you learn to live with it," Lex said. He turned to Robbie in the backseat. "We don't have much time."

The hair on my arm suddenly stood straight up.

Something wasn't right. It was like the barometric pressure had dropped. I glanced out the window to see if a storm was brewing.

But instead of gray clouds, I saw a dark gray fog, and my nose was assaulted by the sticky-sweet smell of the Bborim.

"Um, guys? Do you see that?" I asked as my heart kicked into overdrive. "Do you smell that?"

"Smell what? We best get going now. Ryan is going to start at the historical marker his teacher told him about. He's waiting for dark to go out there, so if we go now, maybe we can find it before he gets there."

"You guys seriously don't see that gray fog? Or smell

the sugar explosion?" I asked, watching the fog trail behind us.

"Work on your exercises," Robbie said. "The Serpentines are just trying to mess with you."

"No. It's really there. I can feel it," I said, taking in a deep breath. I began my mental yoga like Robbie had instructed, but I knew the demon was out there.

"If the demon were there, Lex and I would know."

I tried to relax as Lex pulled away from the curb and headed out of the subdivision. "This marker—how far is it from town?" he asked.

"Fifteen minutes. Take highway seven south. It's on the right a little ways off the road. The shoulder is really wide for parking."

I glanced toward the haunting gray smoke one more time, then closed my eyes and tried to keep the brain brothers out of my head. I couldn't tell if it was working. Usually I felt Lex all up in my mind, and right now he was nowhere to be found. Which could mean that I was getting better. Or it could mean that he was being purposefully quiet.

And I never knew if Robbie was there. That boy must have patented his stealth-warrior mind reading. Hope he made a mint off it.

Robbie chuckled from the backseat. I pulled down the visor and eyed him through the mirror. "Guess that means you're not out of my head, huh?"

"That's what that means. Good news is, you *are* keeping Lex out, so you're getting better."

"Maybe I'm just not trying," Lex said. "Maybe I'm just giving her a break."

Robbie barked with laughter. "Em, yeah. Keep tellin' yerself that, mate."

Lex mumbled something that I couldn't make out, but obviously Robbie heard and nearly doubled over laughing.

"What's so funny?"

Robbie and Lex made eye contact through the rearview mirror. Lex's eyes were broody, but Robbie's were twinkling. It was a little strange seeing their mirror-imaged eyes with such different expressions.

Finally Lex broke the silence. "I'm not used to this, and Robbie is taking great pleasure in my difficulty."

"Used to what?" I asked.

"Truth be told, I've never had anyone successfully block me from their head. Not this quickly. Not like you have. I've been trying since we left Bridget's to get in there, and I've not been successful. It's frustrating."

"Is that it?" I asked.

Lex glanced my way, and a flash of heat mushroomed in my belly. "That's it for now," he said. "We're here."

He pulled the car to the shoulder of the road and parked. As we all got out, I carefully glanced around for any signs of the gray smoke. When I didn't see any, I inhaled deeply. Nothing. Relieved, I joined the brothers at the historical marker. Lex read the engraved words out loud.

"Valley Springs, Mississippi's first settlers built the church in 1792. During an archaeological dig in 1989, other artifacts dating back to the same time period were discovered, as well as evidence that this area was once the location of the original settlement."

Behind the marker was a dirt path that led into a wide clearing in the woods. The sky was turning pink as the sun was beginning to set, and even though there was still quite a bit of light, the farther we followed the path into the woods, the darker it became.

I shuddered and rubbed my arms as a chill cascaded over me.

"You all right, sailor?" Lex wrapped his arm around my shoulders and pulled me closer to him.

"Fine. Just a chill," I said as I tried to rub the unease

away. "So what's our game plan tonight? Look around until we find a rock that looks special? I don't even know what a rune looks like."

"These won't be like the runes that are used for magic today. Usually runes are smaller, with only one symbol or letter etched into them, but the runes we're searching for will be slightly different. They'll be smooth stones, probably palm-size. And when *you* touch them, they should be warm," Robbie said.

"How do you know this?" I asked. "Do they teach you this stuff in Vampire Trainer School?"

They both laughed. "We did learn about the history between Serpentines and Frieceadans—including the falling-out between the two clans and the hiding of the documents. The runes and the scrolls were never to be in the same place," Robbie said.

"What happens if they're brought together again?"

"Nobody's certain. The manipulation of time is what most people believe. It's what the evils want to believe. But the only way to really know what will happen is to get the scrolls and runes together, and nobody wants to do that."

Well, almost nobody. After the Mr. Charles debacle in the fall, we'd searched for the scrolls. We had last seen them in his classroom, but they were nowhere to be found after he disappeared. We could only assume he managed to get them back to the Serpentines. If the Serpentines had both the runes and the scrolls together, who knows what kind of paranormal gate they could open?

I had done a pretty good job of ignoring that everyone believed my father was the one behind this. Which was part of the reason why Ryan no longer trusted me. The burden of knowing that a member of my family could be the one who started all this was almost too much to bear. I hadn't seen or heard from my dad since I was ten years old, but I remembered him as kind, loving, and fun. I didn't want to believe that he had changed, because that meant that if the evil could get to him, then possibly Ryan was right and it could get to me, too.

Maybe I *shouldn't* be trusted.

Well, now we know what we need to work on. Lex's voice in my head startled me. *They'll look for your weaknesses and enter that way. They play on your insecurities. When you feel insecure, you let your guard down. And if I can get back in, so can they.*

I closed my eyes, took a deep breath, and mentally slammed the door to my brain. As soon as I felt alone inside my head, I glanced at Lex. The look on his face was somewhere between shock and awe.

"You're getting good at that. Too bad you can't seem to get rid of Robbie. Better work harder."

I rolled my eyes and flipped Lex off as we rounded a curve on the dirt path. A huge grassy clearing opened up in front of us.

The stone ruins of the old church stood about fifty feet away. The roof was completely gone, as was the majority of the wall on the right side of the building. It was both creepy and beautiful.

"Wow," I said a little breathlessly. "Now what?"

"We start with the trees," Robbie said. "If the runes were hidden here, there will be clues etched in the trees."

"Um, I hate to be an idiot, but what will I be looking for?"

"Trees that are warm to the touch—you're a key holder, so you should feel their energy. The messages will be etched in a crevice or on the roots," Lex said.

"So we're just assuming that after all these years, the etchings will still be there? That the trees are still standing?"

"Sweetheart, you're thinking like a human. These trees are blessed with magic. If the runes are here, the trees are still standing and the clues will be readable," Lex reminded me. "And if you're truly a key holder, you'll find them because you're supposed to."

"Oh yeah. Magic. I spend so much time trying *not* to be magical that I still sometimes forget."

"Here," Robbie said, pulling three small Mag-Lites from his satchel. "I thought we might need these."

We each grabbed a light and split up. I had no idea what I was looking for, but I took Lex at his word and just began to feel the trees. I remembered what the scrolls had felt like when I touched them, how they seemed to hum with a tangible energy that nobody but me could feel or hear. From Lex's description, I should have a similar reaction to the charmed trees.

I took the wall-less side of the church, picked a starting point, and began feeling up some bark.

By tree number fourteen, I was becoming very efficient in bark differentiation. I hopped from tree to tree, feeling for warmth and listening for humming, or whispering, or hoping maybe a squirrel might throw a nut at me or something. Anything. I just needed a sign.

And that's when I tripped on a tree root and busted my ass. Okay, not my ass, my knee. My jeans tore, my skin ripped, and a piercing pain shot up my leg.

"Fuck a duck!" I yelled, biting my lip to refrain from

spitting out many more sailorlike strings of swears. I leaned against the tree, feeling the damp leaves soak through my jeans, and pulled my knee up for closer inspection. This was the second pair of jeans I'd ruined in a week. The torn flesh was already beginning to heal, but it was an ugly gash all the way to the bone. I would be feeling this graceful moment for quite a while.

"You okay, sailor?" Lex called out. "Where are you?"

"I'm fine," I said, pushing myself off the ground. "Just tripped over a tree root, like the essence of grace and beauty that I am."

I had begun to brush the debris from my pants when a flash of red on the tree directly across from me caught my eye. It was a birch tree with a smooth white trunk, and at its base was what appeared to be a red drawing.

"Guys? I may have found something," I yelled as I squatted down to inspect the design a little more closely. It looked like three teardrops intertwined. It was etched into the wood, not drawn. The color was amazing, like it was just freshly done.

I reached down to trace the design, and as soon as my finger touched the symbol, a rush of heat filled me. I closed my eyes and enjoyed the energy as it pulsated through me. My entire body vibrated. It wasn't scary, like the scrolls had been. There were no screams, no panicked cries for help, only a rush of endorphins and warmth.

"Let me see," Robbie demanded.

I pulled back, unable to contain my excitement. It was like a runner's high but without the exhaustion. Lex pulled me out of Robbie's way, and as soon as he touched me, I turned to him, wrapped my arms around his neck, and planted a celebratory kiss on him.

He pulled back with a smile. "I may grow to like not being in your head after all. Surprises are fun."

I winked. "Yep. They can be."

"Fantastic, AJ," Robbie said. "This is exactly what we're looking for. This is a Trinity Knot. Oftentimes we'll see it enclosed in a circle, which tends to mean 'cannot be broken.' I think without the circle we're looking at a much more literal interpretation—the power of three. We're probably looking for three stones.

"Also, the fact that this was drawn on a birch tree is very symbolic. Birch trees were believed to ward off evil and also symbolized new beginnings. I think we need to focus our search on other symbolic trees. Rowan, willow, oak, or ash. Though maybe not oak, just because there are so many here."

"So avoid pine?" I asked.

Robbie laughed. "Yes, avoid pine."

Lex cleared his throat. "Don't really think we need to continue searching," he said, pointing. "Look."

We followed the direction of his finger. Behind the birch and to the right stood a willow tree. And to the left stood a tree I couldn't name.

"Rowan," Robbie answered. "In a triangle."

The rowan tree was marked with a pentagram, another symbol for protection. The willow mark was a horse head. Robbie explained that the horse often symbolized power, guidance, and protection.

"Well, all that's great, but how does this lead us to the runes?" I asked. We had three trees that were warm to the touch, with ancient drawings etched into their bark. It would help if those drawings were maps with an "X" in the middle that said, "Find runes here."

Robbie chuckled, obviously hearing me. "Well, I have two thoughts on where to find the runes. I believe we're looking for three, so it's possible each is buried separately under or hidden in each tree."

"Um, we're not really prepared for that kind of dig," I said.

"No, but neither is Ryan, so at least we're somewhat safe in that respect," Robbie said. "However, he can use magic to help him find them, and if he's skilled enough, it could be a problem for us, especially since there was typically always a Serpentine and a Frieceadan key holder."

"What do you mean?" I asked. "He's a key holder, too?"

"It's a possibility we can't rule out."

Great. Just what I needed. More history tying us together that would probably just eventually rip us apart. "So if you don't think the runes are here, then where?" I asked.

"The kirk," Lex said. "I think it would be too obvious here. Let's try the church first, and if we fail, we come back tomorrow and start digging. I don't think we have to worry about Ryan finding the runes before we do. He doesn't really have anything to go on. And if he is a key holder, he doesn't know it yet."

The sun had fully set now, and even though the sky was more gray than black, the wooded area surrounding the church was dark. Inside the church? Even darker.

There was no longer a door hanging from the hinges. We paused at the threshold and shined our lights inside, scaring a raccoon away. Cobwebs hung like tapestries in every corner. Overall the building was a dilapidated mess, except for the floor.

"It's not even rotting," I said. "How is that possible?"

"Magic," Robbie said. "Lex, you were right. The runes will be in here."

"What are we looking for now?" I asked.

"Another symbol. You feel for warmth," Robbie answered. "Look on the walls, the floor, the dais. We need to check every inch of this building, and do it fast. Ryan will be here soon."

Time had slipped by very quickly. I really didn't want to face Ryan while we were beating him to the punch—it would be much easier afterward to tell him we had the runes, how we got them, why destroying them was a bad idea, and prove to him that we weren't going to use them for evil.

We fanned out, each of us taking a section of the small church. I took the pulpit area, which was more like a small stage. I searched the floor, the walls, even the spiderwebs. Nothing.

No heat, no humming, no etchings, no runes.

"I'm going to check out the wall-less side, just in case there's something left to investigate."

"Good idea," Lex said. "I've found a couple of other symbols and some Gaelic, but they're red herrings. Still, the runes have to be here somewhere."

I took my time, shining the light along the edge of the remaining wall, pulling vines off, brushing more thready spiderwebs out of my way. No heat. No humming. No symbols.

I sat on the broken wall, which was about knee high in height, and shined the light along the outside. Maybe they had hidden the runes among the stones on the outside of the wall instead of the inside.

I did my best Winnie-the-Pooh impression. *Think, think, think.* I cleared my mind and tried to channel the spirit of the runes. Okay, not really.

A light breeze blew a pretty purple flower against my leg, and a sudden warmth filled me. Then a gentle buzzing began. "Um, Robbie. Does this purple flower mean anything to you?" I asked. "Because it started humming when I touched it."

Chapter 12

obbie and Lex leaped over the wall to inspect the flower. "It's a thistle, the national Scottish flower," Robbie said.

"Thistle. Brilliant. Never would've thought to search for that. Good on ya, sailor," Lex said.

"Did they bury the runes? Or put them in the wall?" I asked.

"They buried them. How did you find this?" Lex asked.

"It was an accident. Just like the tree."

"No such thing as an accident where this is concerned. You were supposed to find it," Robbie said. "Now, let's hope they're not buried too far down so we can find them and get the hell out before Ryan gets here."

Lex bent down and pulled the thistle up by its roots, untangling a small, dirt-covered bag. "The bugger is tied up in these roots. Amazing."

Lex stopped fiddling with the bag for a second and cocked his head toward the road. "Shit. Ryan's here, and he's got Bridget with him."

"He really brought Bridget? What about Oz and Rayden?" I asked.

"I don't think the lads are with him now. I don't hear them on the trail, anyway."

"I can't have this discussion in front of Bridget," I said. "And I really don't want to face Ryan right now. Not here."

"Probably should've thought about that before we parked on the street, sailor," Lex said, stuffing the bag into his jeans pocket.

"I'm going to go through the woods so they won't see me," Robbie said. "Bridget would believe you two were out here alone. She'd be a little curious about the three of us."

"See you in a few, mate," Lex said as Robbie stealthily took off through the woods. "He's not much of a fighter, but the lad is crazy quiet. Like his feet are clouds."

"Okay, so what are we going to tell them when they get here? We need to get our stories straight, and then later, when we have Ryan alone, we can tell him everything."

Lex stepped back up into the chapel. "We're not going to say one word about why we're here. They'll be able to figure it out all by themselves."

He switched off his flashlight, laid it on the wall, grabbed me by my waist, and pushed me against the nearest full wall. "I like not being in your head," he said. "Because now I can surprise you, too."

Lex's palm was warm on my neck as he brushed my hair off my shoulder. With the barest touch of his fingertip, he traced my birthmark, sending chills crashing over my body. My breathing quickened along with my heart as I waited for him to kiss me. Or touch me. Or do whatever it was he wanted to do.

The anticipation was torture. I bit my bottom lip and did everything in my power to stop from grabbing his head and pulling him to me.

With a slow, cocky smile, Lex lowered his lips until they were a whisper away from mine. For a moment I thought I would die from waiting. But then he put me out of my misery with a featherlike kiss that weakened my knees. I leaned into the wall, thankful for its support, and just breathed into him.

I gave myself over to the kiss. Lex's lips were soft, warm, and he tasted like an atomic fireball.

I felt like modeling clay in his arms.

Lex moved his hand from my neck, through my hair, then down to the small of my back, creating another round of chills. I wrapped my arms tightly around his neck, pulling him as close to me as possible.

I completely forgot about Ryan and Bridget.

I didn't hear them approach the church or see the beam of light from their flashlight. So when I heard the floor creak under their weight, I was so startled I gasped.

The light immediately blinded me as Ryan pointed it in my face. "What the hell?" he asked. "AJ? What are you doing here?"

"Would you like a play-by-play?" Lex asked.

I pinched him under the arm and muttered, "Not helpful."

"Um, hey," I said, thankful for the bad lighting. My cheeks were burning hot, and I wasn't sure if it was from the kiss, getting busted, or the heat of Ryan's glare.

"What's the deal?" Ryan demanded.

I had originally planned to just apologize, skirt any

questions, and get the hell out of Dodge, but Ryan's tone had my back up. "I think it's kinda obvious why we're here, Ryan. We were tired of having an audience at home. And you?"

I glanced at Bridget, who seemed a little shell-shocked. She was twirling her hair and not saying a word.

"We're doing some extra-credit work for Mrs. Christopher," Ryan said.

"Together?" I asked. "Did I miss it when Mrs. Christopher assigned partners?" Okay, so I was being a little petty, but dammit, my best friend went to my ex-boyfriend-now-brother instead of me.

Bridget shuffled from side to side nervously but didn't say anything.

"This is something outside of class, which is why it's called extra credit. Too bad you can't get points every time you two are together. You'd have a six-point-oh GPA by now." Ryan's voice was full of jealousy.

Lex smirked, placed his palm on my back again, and eased me toward the door. "You kids don't do anything I wouldn't do."

The anger on Ryan's face practically glowed in the darkness. Half of me wished I had Lex's ability to listen to Ryan's private thoughts, and the other half was thankful I couldn't hear it. I bet Ryan's creative string of words put my sailorness to shame.

It did.

Dammit! I let my guard down. "How long have you been in there?"

"Long enough to know you were jealous," Lex said as we followed the path to the car. He never moved his hand from my back.

"I'm not jealous! I'm mad that Bridget doesn't think she can come to me. And I'm really mad at Ryan for his attitude."

Lex stopped, taking both of my hands in his. "It's all right, love. I told you, I like complicated. And challenges."

"I'm not jealous."

"You might be a smidge now, but give me a little time and that boy will be just a fond memory."

Lex pulled me to him and kissed me softly. I wanted to enjoy the kiss, but all I could really do was concentrate on getting Lex out of my head so I could think alone.

Just as I was beginning to relax enough to really give in to the kiss, that nauseating smell surrounded me. It was like being punched in the stomach.

I pulled away.

"The Bborim is here."

Robbie got out of the car. "AJ, the Serpentines are just messing with your head."

"No. I'm telling you. It's here."

A gray fog began to form and thicken, surrounding us in that nauseating bubblegummy smell.

"You should listen to her," the scratchy voice came from the fog, but nobody appeared. "She knows what she's talking about."

Lex pressed me between himself and the car as his eyes darted around to see if he could locate the beast.

"There's no need to protect her from me, vampire trainer. She's family."

The smell was overwhelming me now, and the more the demon talked, the more nauseated I became. I began to feel feverish, with burning skin followed by chills.

"Have you figured it out?" the invisible demon asked. "Do you know why you can see me before the others? Why you smell me first?"

"Enlighten me," I said.

"Because you're special. The others aren't like you, AJ—you have a gift, and your real family needs you now."

I opened my mouth to answer, but before I had a chance to say anything, I felt the car move behind me, like it was under a great weight. I tensed up to react, but I wasn't fast enough.

A meaty hand appeared out of nowhere, wrapping around my arm and pulling me off the ground like I was a feather.

I screamed as Lex and Robbie flew toward us. I was flailing, trying to slip free from the demon's ironclad grip. Its gravelly laughter echoed in my head at my weak attempt. I finally managed to free an arm and quickly punched the demon in the throat. But instead of letting me go, the demon pulled my arm right out of the socket.

I went limp as pain seared through my shoulder. I didn't pass out exactly, but I was damn near close.

Robbie flew at the beast from behind, slamming into us feet first. It was a powerful hit that knocked the Bborim down a bit, which meant it yanked my arm down with it, sending a whole new round of pain through my body.

"What do you want from me?" I asked, hoping to distract it while Lex and Robbie attacked.

"The runes. I want you to find the runes."

Lex came at the demon with his fangs bared. The Bborim grabbed me by the waist with its other arm and held me in front like a shield, bringing Lex to a screeching halt.

"I don't want to hurt her, but I will."

While my arm was out of its socket, I was pretty much useless. It hurt to think about moving, so trying to actually get away would take me from this state of semiconsciousness to flat-out comatose.

"Just give me the runes and I'll let her go," the demon bargained.

"Yeah, I'll get right on that," Lex replied. He looked over at Robbie and nodded slightly.

I didn't see Robbie as he dove toward me, but I felt him. He swooped in quickly, silently, and just plucked me out of the demon's hands. And that's when he and Lex went after blood.

A car squealed to a halt on the road and pox-covered Mr. Charles popped out, his eyes a bit wild. He reminded me of a hyped-up cartoon character.

I heard a grunt and glanced over to see Robbie flat on his back in the road. Lex and the demon were still going at it. Robbie didn't stay down long, but he was moving considerably more slowly than before.

Mr. Charles grabbed me by the arm, and pain again seared across my shoulder as he pulled me to him. "Don't worry," Mr. Charles said. "I'll save you!"

Did he actually believe he was being heroic?

My fangs descended, and heat spread across my face.

"The only thing you better hope to save is yourself!" I yelled as I chomped down on his neck. I concentrated hard so I wouldn't release any venom. No way in hell was I going to fulfill this asshole's dream of becoming a vampire. But I would gladly take some of his blood to help regain my strength.

By the way, pustule-saturated blood tastes like crap.

Mr. Charles squealed. "That hurts! But the pain is worth it!"

I stopped sucking and spat. "I'm not changing you, dumbass. I'm just weakening you."

"What—?" he started to say but was very rudely interrupted by my knee in his crotch. He doubled over, gasping for air.

Mr. Charles didn't get a chance to nurse his injury long before Robbie picked him up by the scruff and tossed him away like he was a bag of trash.

Mr. Charles didn't try to save the day again. He limped over to the car as fast as he could, jumped in, and locked the door. He tried to start the car, but the engine wouldn't turn.

Mr. Charles cracked open the window. "Finish him off," he yelled at the Bborim.

The demon roared in response, grabbing Lex by the neck, but Lex was too wily and managed to slip out of its grip.

Robbie looked at me. "Are you okay?"

"Yeah. I'm good. Except I need some mouthwash now. Bleh."

"Glad it didn't hurt you too much. And by the way, I'm sorry to have to do this."

That was the only warning he gave me before he shoved my arm back into place.

If I thought having my arm popped out of the socket was painful, it was nothing compared to the agony of having it crammed back in.

Thank God for quick healing. I rotated my shoulder to make sure it worked properly, then said, "Let's go kick some demon ass."

"Lex has it. We'll jump in if we have to, but right now, you're staying away from that thing and I'm staying right here with you."

"Then you can come with me to finish dealing with Mr. Charles."

I started toward the car, and Mr. Charles's eyes went wide. In a rushed panic, he turned the engine over and over. I thought he was going to flood the car, which would have worked to my advantage, but the bubble-covered dipwad had a stroke of luck. When the engine finally rumbled to life, he peeled out like a street racer.

I heard a loud crunch and spun to see that Lex and the demon had moved the fight to the hood of my car. I wondered if my insurance covered damage caused by paranormal beings.

Lex got in a roundhouse kick to the face, knocking the demon to the ground, and even though the beast was double his size, Lex managed to dive in and sink his teeth into the Bborim's side.

But not for long. The demon plucked Lex up and tossed him into a tree. Then the demon flew toward Lex with its giant fangs glistening.

It was pissed.

But Lex was ready. He jumped to the first branch of the tree, ripped off a limb, and rammed it right into the demon's thigh.

The Bborim's high-pitched shriek was heard around the world. And then the creature evaporated into thin air.

Chapter 13

We left quick, fast, and in a hurry before the Bborim decided to come back. I called Ryan to warn him, but he didn't answer his phone.

"He'll be safe tonight. That thing wants you because it knows you're a key holder. It doesn't suspect Ryan could be one as well. Besides, it was injured and weakened, so it won't be back this evening," Lex said.

"I hope you're right."

"Are you okay, sailor?" Lex asked.

"Fine." My voice sounded distant, even to me. I rubbed my shoulder and stared out the window.

Are you sure?

Robbie drove while Lex and I sat in the backseat.

As soon as Lex whispered into my mind, I shut the door again. Lex pulled away a little. Like me closing off my thoughts was equal to shutting him out.

And maybe I was in a way. I was so overwhelmed. On top of being the target of some crazed demon, I had my real-life teenage drama to add to it.

Ryan was single but unavailable. Bridget and Malia, my two best friends since forever, seemed to hate each other. And now Bridget was spending private time with Ryan—in a dark building where God only knows what could happen.

Not that anything would happen. Bridget was still crazy about Grady. Right?

I reflexively licked the lingering taste of cinnamon from my lips. I knew damn good and well what could happen in that building. Lex had kissed me stupid back there. So stupid that I had forgotten that Ryan was in the same county, much less on his way to walking in on us.

So stupid that I had forgotten the kiss was all for show.

Disappointment fluttered in my belly. This whole thing was confusing. Lex had always been nothing but a player, but I sure enjoyed every moment of his game. He touched me like I was a rare silk. He looked at me like I was his last meal. And he kissed me like I tasted better than nectar.

How hard was it for him, though? Getting bored with every girl because he knew what she was thinking before she did? Sure, it would be fun at first, but I couldn't imagine living with no surprises. I thought maybe I'd changed his game a little. And I liked that idea a lot.

Now he had just saved me from being kidnapped by the Bborim. He'd risked his life for me. I had to admit, it sure was sexy the way he protected me, even if it was a little Cro-Magnon.

I had reached to unbuckle my seat belt and slide over next to him when my cell phone rang. I fished it out of my pocket. It was Auntie Tave.

"AJ, there's been a terrible accident. You need to get to the hospital. Immediately. And call Ryan."

"What's happened?" I asked, panic burning my throat.

"It's your mom and Rick. I'll explain everything when you get here."

I don't even know when Lex slid next to me and wrapped me up in his arms, but his warmth comforted me. I ended the call and dialed Ryan immediately. He didn't answer. Again. I tried him and Bridget several times. Nothing. I left voice mails.

"Call Doreen and ask her to call Ryan," Lex said. "He won't ignore her."

"Good idea," I said as I dialed. She answered on the first ring.

"Hello." Her voice was weary.

"Aunt D, it's AJ. I'm on my way to the hospital, but I can't get Ryan to answer his phone to tell him. Can you call his cell phone for me?"

"Of course, dearie. And ye be careful, ye hear?"

"Yes, ma'am. Do you know details?" I asked.

"They're both in surgery. Tha's all I ken."

I closed my phone and blinked away the hot tears that burned my eyelids. "They're in surgery," I said.

Lex kissed my forehead. "Let's wait 'til we get there to worry, love."

I leaned into him and closed my eyes. I tried to release the worry balled up in the pit of my stomach, but all I could picture was losing my family. And wondering what it would be like to face the world without the people I loved the most.

Including Ryan. Because if the worst did happen and we lost both of our parents, that would permanently split the earth between Ryan and me, all the way to the bedrock. The damage would be irreparable.

Robbie dropped Lex and me off at the door, then went to park. We hurried to the elevators, which seemed slower than ever. When one finally opened for us, I punched the fifth-floor button and hoped the damn thing would suddenly develop warp speed.

By the time the elevator stopped, I had almost chewed my thumbnail to the quick. Auntie Tave was waiting for us.

I rushed into her open arms and let her hold me while I tried to get hold of myself. Panicking wouldn't do me any good. And it wouldn't change things.

"What are the details?" I asked. "Aunt D said they're in surgery. What happened?"

Auntie Tave took my hand and walked me to the waiting room as Robbie got off the elevator. He and Lex followed behind.

"There was a car accident. We're not really sure what happened. Maybe a hit-and-run, but we're not positive. After you called me earlier, I phoned Rick and he came to the hospital to make sure your mom got home safely. They weren't far from the house when it happened. There were no witnesses. Somebody just happened by the car after the fact. It was smoking and upside down. They had to be cut out."

"Mom and the baby?" I choked on my words.

"The baby is being delivered now by emergency C-section. Liz was almost eight months pregnant, so unless something really bad happened during the accident, the baby should be fine. But your mother has lost a lot of blood, AJ. And with what her body has been through with the pregnancy, it's not looking good."

My knees buckled, and Lex stopped me from just collapsing to the floor. He walked me over to a chair and forced me to sit.

"What about Rick?" Lex asked.

"He had some trauma to the head. He's in surgery to release the swelling. They are cautiously optimistic about his recovery, but he will be in the hospital for a while."

Ryan walked into the waiting room just as Tave was talking about Rick. As soon as Tave saw him, she backed up to the beginning—to where Mom left the house because she couldn't stop herself.

His eyes widened in shock.

After the information registered with him, Ryan turned on me.

"This is your fault," he said. "You brought those

bastards to us. If I lose my dad, I'll never forgive you."

"Ryan!" Auntie Tave said. "I know you're upset, but don't say things you'll regret."

Bridget walked in then, but Ryan just grabbed her by the arm and pulled her out.

My mouth was suddenly like sand as the crack between us grew wider. Couldn't he have at least waited until our parents were out of surgery before he attacked me?

A doctor I didn't recognize came into the waiting room.

"Hello, Octavia. Is this Dr. Fraser's daughter?" he asked.

"It is. AJ, this is Dr. Douglas. He was your mother's surgeon today. And he's fully aware of her special condition."

Code for "He's one of us."

"The baby is doing well. She was a little over seven pounds and came out screaming bloody murder. We have her in the NICU for the time being, but I think she'll be moved soon."

"And Mom?" I asked with a cracking voice.

"She lost a lot of blood. The accident caused an abruption, which is why we had to deliver your sister so early. And because of her already tenuous circumstances, this extra blood loss has really taken its toll on her. She's extremely weak and still in critical condition."

Lex wrapped his hand around mine as I sat there dazed. "Can I see her?"

"Soon. ICU has visitation every three hours. Next one coming up is at nine."

"Can I see my sister?"

"Absolutely," he said.

"Is there any word on Liz's husband, Rick?" Auntie Tave asked.

"I can check, but it will probably be a little while longer. Octavia, can you show AJ to the NICU?" Dr. Douglas asked.

"Yes, thanks, Jim. For everything," Tave said as Dr. Douglas left the waiting room. "We need to tell Ryan about the baby," she said to me. "He should come see her."

We all walked down the fluorescent hallway, which felt a little like walking toward the electric chair. Ryan and Bridget seemed lost in conversation as they stood next to the vending machines.

"Ryan," Octavia said. "Your baby sister is in the NICU. We're headed down to see her and thought you might want to join us."

His dark eyes turned to ice as he glared at me. "I'll go later. Thanks."

I tried to swallow the painful lump that had formed in my throat. "We're still family, Ryan," I said. "No matter how you feel about me right now, the fact is, we're still family. We're all in this together."

"Sorry, *sis*. This isn't an 'all for one and one for all' moment. You worry about your family and I'll worry about mine."

"C'mon, love. Let's go see your sister while duffer here acts like a selfish git." Lex entwined his fingers with mine and pulled me away. I was shaking like a kitten caught in the rain, but holding Lex's hand helped calm me a little. I was so grateful I had him to lean on right now.

"Ryan will come around," Auntie Tave said. "Some people really don't know how to handle stress, so they lash out at those they love."

I tried to stop the laughter when I felt it bubbling in my chest, but I couldn't. It escaped in a loud hoot, and I was powerless against it. I laughed until I was gasping for breath and tears were streaming down my face.

"*Love,*" I mocked with an eye roll. "Yeah. Ryan's all about the love, isn't he? Sorry, Tave. I know you mean well, but he's in a really bad place, and frankly, he can stay there. Alone. Or, if Bridget wants to go there with him, more power to her. But he's not dragging me into his drama. I need to make sure everyone is healthy, and then I plan to keep them that way. With or without his help."

Auntie Tave looked at me with big, sad eyes. "I just don't understand what happened," she said.

"It started out as jealousy because of Lex and me, but it's turned into something much more," I answered. "He's basically of the mind that we vampires should stick to our own kind."

The look of shock on Tave's face was priceless. "Surely you're exaggerating," she said. But instead of looking at me, she looked at Robbie and Lex for confirmation.

Both shook their heads no.

Tave seemed to lose herself in thought as we continued on our way to the NICU. I leaned in closer to Lex and worked on keeping Robbie out of my head. I think I finally figured out how to tell when he was in there. When Lex was in there it was obvious; it was a physical sensation, like he was pounding on a door to get inside. Robbie was so different. He was quiet and unassuming in real life, which meant he was exactly the same way in empath life. He was like an electronic bug in a room, hidden so well that he could only be found by accident.

Which is exactly how I discovered him. I had noticed in the car that even though I shut the door to Lex, something was still there. Something small but noticeable. Like a tack on the floor. Nobody sees it until they step on it. But once they step on it, they can't believe they missed it.

I must have stepped on Robbie in my head as I shut out Lex. And I'd been focusing on getting him the hell out of my head ever since. I wanted to be alone in my own skin again, thank-you-very-much.

The NICU was on the same floor, but it seemed to be fourteen miles away from where we had been. We arrived at the secured area, got our family wristbands, and after what seemed like forever, finally got to see the baby.

She was in this plastic incubator thing, connected to an IV and heart monitor. She had a shocking full head of black hair. All the Ashe girls had blond hair.

Oh. Right. She wasn't an Ashe girl. She was a Fraser. Well, technically, she was an Ashe-Fraser.

A tear slid down my cheek as I watched her little chest move up and down, working for every breath. Where did she fit into this fractured family?

Poor thing. So weak, so tiny, and born into such turmoil.

That's when it dawned on me. She was here. Alive. And unprotected.

"Oh no," I said. "She's not at home. She's not in the house. She's not protected."

Octavia nodded. "Someone will have to stay with her twenty-four/seven."

"Is there some protective spell Aunt D can cast to help?"

"Yes, but she'll have to do it later. When there aren't so many people around."

That's when I realized that with all the drama, we hadn't told Tave about our latest brush with the Bborim.

"Auntie Tave, you might want to get Aunt D up here as quickly as possible. We were attacked again tonight. Nobody's safe right now. Nobody."

Chapter 14

Rick came through his surgery fine. They expected a full recovery, provided there were no complications. He would be in the hospital for a few days while he recovered.

I wasn't really worried about Rick. Something inside me told me he'd be okay. But Momma? I didn't have the same confident attitude.

Her body was not responding to any of the transfusions. It was like she was refusing the blood. Like maybe her body thought it was water instead.

But even though her vitals were weak, they were steady. And steady was good. If we could just get her to accept the blood, life would be okay. *Her* life would be okay.

Lex and Robbie dropped me off at the house a little after midnight. Aunt D and I were two ships passing in the night, as she was just headed to the hospital to cast some major protection juju on the baby.

Robbie and Lex followed me into the kitchen. I went immediately to the fridge, grabbed three hemoshakes, and passed them out. We were all famished.

And exhausted.

I took a long pull from my drink and almost grimaced.

"Once you've tasted real blood, these hemoshakes just don't quite do the trick, do they, sailor?" Lex asked.

"Tastes better than Mr. Charles's blood, though," I said with a laugh.

But he was right. The hemoshakes were almost bland compared to the velvety richness of real blood. And I wanted to taste it again.

Actually, I wanted to taste *his* blood again.

But there was no time for that right now. We had more important stuff to talk about. Like the runes that we hadn't even looked at yet.

We all took a seat at the island in the middle of the kitchen, with our cans of fake V8, and wearily watched as Lex pulled the dirty brown package from his pocket and untied it.

He dumped the contents between us. There were several stones, some gravel, and one palm-sized smooth black rock with some weird lettering on it.

"There's only one," Robbie said, confusion clear in his voice. "There should be three, but there is only one."

"Maybe there was only one to begin with," I offered.

Lex picked up the rune and studied it. "No. There are at least two more. This one is marked 'tra,' which is three."

"Do we need to go back and look again?" I asked.

"No. They're not there. I'm sure we would've been guided to them if they were. We just have to keep looking. And we can't let Ryan get to them first," Robbie said.

Sadness shadowed my heart with his words. The one person I used to trust the most was now public enemy number one. Or maybe public enemy number two. I was pretty sure the demon was first on the list. At least for now.

Robbie looked at me and smiled. "You did good today. Blocking me, that is. I couldn't get in for about two hours. And that was during stress. So you're getting there."

"Thanks. You've taught me well. Now, if I could just keep the bastards out of my head at night."

"Is it getting better?" Lex asked.

"Somewhat. But they're still there. I can always feel them. They might not be knocking on my door, but they're definitely looking through my windows, and I don't like it."

"We're staying here tonight," Lex said. "There's no telling when Doreen will be home, and you guys aren't going to be here alone. We'll sleep in the living room, so don't worry about your virtue." He winked. "It's completely safe with me."

"Good to know," I said with a laugh. "Actually, I'm glad you're staying. This whole thing has me on edge."

Lex put the rune back in his pocket and walked me upstairs to my room.

"There are linens in the closet under the stairs," I said, suddenly nervous. "Anything you'll need to keep warm."

His smile was slow and lazy as he propped himself against my door frame. "You could keep me warm."

My belly flipped. "Good thing I know you're just playing with me to get a reaction, Alexander Archer."

His chuckle was low, throaty, and melt-in-your-mouth sexy. "You know that for sure, do you?"

I stood on my tiptoes and brushed my lips against his. "I do. Because no matter how much you play at being a bad boy, you're a good guy at heart. And you would never try to seduce me while my mother was fighting for her life. Plus, I'm barely eighteen."

His eyes went from playful to serious in a split second. "You know all that about me, do you?" he asked.

"Am I wrong?"

"No. What gave me away?"

I reached up, cupping his face in my hands. "The eyes. They give everyone away." I touched my lips to his. He responded with a sigh.

"Good night, kitten," I said, smiling as I closed the door to my room.

"Just so you know, I have no trouble with your age," he said.

I leaned against the door and listened to Lex's footsteps as he went back downstairs. I heard the linen closet door open and shut, and just as I was walking away from the door, I heard Lex mutter, "You had to get tangled up in a smart one, didn't you, Archer, you stupid git."

I smiled. Alexander Archer might be one helluva tough guy and vampire trainer, but he was a powder puff at heart. And I liked that about him.

The dreams came at me like a runaway train: full speed and out of control.

I couldn't tell what was real, what was imagined, and what images were being forced on me.

Panic seized me as I lay in my bed completely paralyzed, in a state of semiconsciousness. I couldn't stop the images flashing in my head.

I was being crowned queen in front of a faceless crowd. I was happy, enjoying the moment. And then the lights panned across the audience and all I could see were fangs and blood. Everywhere.

Suddenly I was gasping for breath. Trying to figure out what had happened. Did I betray my family? Myself? Did I rejoin the Serpentines?

I wanted to let out a scream, but it was stuck in my throat. I wanted to run, but my feet were stuck to the floor. Stuck. That was exactly what I was.

Wake up, love. Wake up. It's just a dream.

Lex's voice was a light in the darkness. I couldn't see where it was coming from, but I could feel it. It offered warmth and protection, so I latched on and followed it.

That a girl. *C'mon. Follow me.*

I didn't know where I was going; I just knew this was the right path. *Keep talking.*

I had a dream about you last night, sailor. We were on the beach, holding hands, watching the sunset over the ocean. Your eyes matched the water. To quote a song, they were deep-blue, need-you eyes, and I couldn't stop staring into them.

My heart was racing, but I was no longer scared. *Tell me more.*

He paused. *I think you're the first girl I want to introduce to my mum.*

And with that, I was no longer paralyzed in my bed. I wiggled my feet, moved my legs, and opened my eyes.

Lex was sitting on the side of the bed, staring at me intently. I blinked away the sleep and confusion and tried to get my bearings.

"You all right?" he asked. "That was some dream."

"You could see it?" I asked.

"I could. Woke me right up when I thought I was being crowned. I don't look good in tiaras—not that I've ever worn one before." He laughed and winked at me.

"I've been doing so well keeping you out of my head. Why now?"

"When you go to sleep, you have less control over your subconscious. It just takes some more training. That's all. I know you can do it. You're already blocking Robbie, which is amazing. So don't worry, love. You'll be fine."

I sat up and rubbed my face. The sky was slowly turning to gray as dawn was creeping to the surface. His words nestled into a small corner of my heart and warmed me. But as much as I wanted to explore the whole mum thing, we currently had more urgent things to tackle.

Resolve took hold of me like a vise grip.

"We have to find the other two runes," I said. "Where are we going to start?"

"We'll figure it out tomorrow," Lex said, pulling the rune from his inside jacket pocket. "It's as cold as ice to me. Is it still warm when you touch it?"

I took it from him and heat filled my palm. And then suddenly I saw the second rune in my head. It was like looking at a picture in an album. "It's trying to tell me where the second rune is," I said.

"What do you mean?" Lex asked.

"I mean, when I hold the stone, a picture of another rune flashes in my head. They're trying to communicate with me. Or with each other. The rune isn't buried, but I can't tell where it is."

"Let's sort it out at breakfast. I bet we can figure it out together."

"Sounds good."

Lex lifted his hand to my hair, pushing it away from my face. "You okay now, sailor?" he asked.

I placed my hand over his and smiled. "Better.

Thanks for waking me."

"That's what we bodyguards do," he said with a sad laugh.

"You're definitely one of the good guys, Lex Archer."

"So you keep saying. But even good guys have their limits. I better leave now or else I'll be risking my virtue as well as yours." He gently popped the strap of my tank top and winked at me.

I swatted his hand away sleepily. "I'm going to shower, then I'll be downstairs. We can go on the great rune hunt after we check on Mom, Rick, and the baby."

Lex stopped at the doorway and turned back to me with a slow smile. "I'll be taking a shower as well. A long, cold one."

"Shut up." I threw a pillow at him, which he easily dodged.

"Guess I know what we'll be working on at our next training," he said.

"What's that?"

"Target practice."

"You're funny." I rolled my eyes as he walked away.

"Uh-oh," he said from the hallway. "Brace yourself, sailor."

I slid out of bed and wrapped the comforter around

me to go see what Lex was talking about. Before I got to the hall, I heard Ryan's angry voice.

"Unbelievable."

I stood in the doorway and watched the two guys in my life glare at each other on the stairs. Ryan looked at Lex, then over at me. "Maybe he should've slithered out of your room a little earlier, AJ."

"Ryan, it wasn't like that. I had one of my nightmares and he woke me." Even though I didn't owe him an explanation, I wanted to give him one.

"I thought the nightmares had stopped," he accused. "And honestly, AJ, how could he have known you were having nightmares unless he was in here with you? I'm across the hall and I don't hear you. I thought he had to be in the vicinity for his Jedi mind trick to work."

How could I explain it? Ever since my training, the dreams had stopped—I'd been sleeping like the dead. But yesterday's mental exertion and battle with Tall, Dark, and Ugly must have drained me. I wasn't strong enough to keep them away.

"He was downstairs and got pulled into my dream with me," I said.

"I like how you're using his mind trick as a cover. Very smart."

"Listen, mate. It's not like that," Lex said. "Why don't you just calm down? You're worried about your family, you've been up all night, and you're just a little punchy right now. Get some sleep, then let's all talk this afternoon. We have a lot to discuss."

Ryan clenched his jaw. I could almost see the steam pluming from his ears. "You're not my family, you're not my *mate*, and you don't belong in my house. Get out." He nearly spat the words at Lex.

"Grow up, kid," Lex said as he tried to pass Ryan on the stairs.

That sent Ryan over the edge. He shoved Lex hard in the chest, knocking him backward.

"Ryan!" I yelled. "What the hell?"

A strange look flitted over Ryan's face, then immediately he masked it.

"Feel better now?" Lex asked.

Ryan smiled, and suddenly he seemed very calm. "I do feel better, actually. I'm outta here," he said as he turned and started back down the stairs. "Later."

"What was that about?" I asked.

"I'm not sure. His mind went blank just after he shoved me. But I can tell you one thing, sailor. Wherever he's going, we need to beat him there."

"I *have* to go to the hospital. If you want to follow him, go for it, but my family comes first."

"Okay, I'll go after Ryan. If I find out anything, I'll call you."

Lex and Robbie took off after Ryan like bloodhounds hot on a trail.

Aunt D called to tell me she'd be home soon and asked if I'd wait for her. I took a long shower and tried desperately to wash the stress away.

I let the kids sleep in since we wouldn't be going to school today. They hadn't been to the hospital yet, and now that everyone was out of surgery they could finally go visit.

The kitchen was filled with early-morning sun and the smell of fresh coffee. Thank the java gods for automatic brewing. I wasn't sure what I needed more right now, a shot of hemoglobin or espresso.

I pulled a hemoshake from the fridge, downing it without tasting it as I poured my first cup of wake-up.

"Now, what to eat for real breakfast."

Just as I began to forage for food, I heard a knock on the kitchen door. I grabbed a key-lime yogurt out of the fridge, then turned to see who was there, fully expecting it to be Bridget or Malia.

I promptly dropped my yogurt, splattering the floor, the fridge, and the wall with blobs of spring green.

It wasn't one of my friends.

It was my father.

Chapter 15

Clive Ashe stared at me through the window. He hadn't aged much since I had last seen him. His short, almost white blond hair was just slightly thin at the temples, his teeth were perfectly straight, his blue eyes were so vivid they practically twinkled, and even though he was smiling at me, my blood ran cold.

I hadn't seen this man in almost eight years. And until the whole you-might-be-a-venomous-Serpentine thing came up last year, I had barely thought about him. What thoughts I had had since then hadn't been that complimentary.

During my angry-teen phase, I used to imagine all the awful things I would say to him if I ever saw him again.

I'd have pretend conversations in my head (okay, out loud), and I would tell him off in the best way a thirteen-year-old girl knew how.

I can honestly say that the things running through my head right now put that thirteen-year-old to shame and definitely earned me the sailor nickname.

"Ariel Jane, I know this is probably weird."

"Go away," I said, walking to the sink. I grabbed the dishrag and began to clean up my key-lime mess.

"You're just so grown up. You look just like your mother. I'm so sorry I wasn't here for you."

"Sorry would've been great a few years ago. Now it's just sad," I replied coolly as I wiped up the green. Okay, I scrubbed one section of the floor. There was tons of yogurt all over the place, but I seemed to only be able to concentrate on one floorboard.

"AJ, listen. The hospital called me. I know about the accident. I know that you don't have anyone to help take care of you and your sisters. I'm here to help. I'm sorry. It was crappy what I did. But I'm here now. Let me make it up to you."

"Go to hell."

I turned my back to him, unwilling to let him in the house. If I let him in my kitchen, then I was letting him back into my life. And he was not welcome in my life again. Ever.

Not just because he abandoned us. That was bad, but not necessarily unforgivable. But my gut said that he was involved with that whole Mr. Charles disaster last year. That he had sent that man after me and a dichampyr to stalk me and threaten the people I love most. For all I know, my father was the man responsible for turning Noah into a dichampyr in the first place.

He was not allowed in my house. Or in my life.

I finally stopped cleaning the one section of the floor and moved on to the rest of the mess. Little green blobs were dotted in random patterns on the barstools, the bar, the fridge, and my shoes. As I was wiping away the last of the goop, the kitchen door opened.

"Oh, hello dearie. Let me put my bag down and I'll finish cleaning this right up for ye."

I jumped at the sound of Aunt D's voice. I looked over her shoulder to see if Clive was still out there. Nothing. Relief flooded my bloodstream. "That's okay, Aunt D. I'm finished now." I threw the yogurt cup in the trash and walked to the sink to rinse out the rag. "Was there anyone in the driveway when you came home?"

"No. Should there have been?"

"No. Just curious. Thought maybe Bridget or Malia would drop by before school."

"Are ye okay?" Aunt D asked. "Ye seem a little peaked. I can whip ye up some hemo-eggs if you need a little extra iron."

I smiled. Ever since Aunt D had been introduced to hemoshakes, she'd been creating all sorts of new vampire-friendly recipes. Some were good. The hemo-eggs? Not so much.

"I'm just tired. You know, long night and all. Are you going to take the kids to the hospital later?" I had to stay focused. I couldn't let the sudden reappearance of daddy-do-wrong shake me. I wouldn't let him get to me.

"Aye. After I kip a wink or two. Ye going to the hospital now?"

"Yes, ma'am. Are they all . . ." I hesitated for a second, "okay?"

"So far, so good. The bairn is strong. She'll be out of intensive care soon. Rick is doing better. He woke up and spoke to Ryan for a few minutes this morning."

"And Mom?"

Aunt D patted my cheek. "She's hangin' in. Go see her; ye'll feel better."

◊◊◊

Dr. Douglas was in Mom's room when I arrived. His brow was furrowed as he checked out her chart.

"Is it bad?" I asked.

He started at my question but recovered quickly. "Hello, AJ," he said with a smile. "I'll be honest—it's not great. We can't seem to give her enough blood, and I have no idea why."

I took a deep breath and summoned up enough courage to look at her. She was pale—very pale. And the bruising on her arms and face made her look even more so.

She seemed so small and frail in the bed. I had to fight the tears as I picked up her wrist and felt her thready pulse with my fingers.

I blinked away the tears that threatened. I had to be strong. Not just for Momma, but for everyone in the family. Especially since Daddy Dearest was back in the picture. Or at least trying to be back in the picture.

"What can we do?" I asked.

"Pray," he said. "I'm sorry, AJ. We've done all we can. We just have to hope her body will start accepting the blood soon."

Dr. Douglas left the room. Not exactly what I was hoping to hear. Not even close, actually.

"I'm sorry you're having to deal with this, Ariel."

I didn't have to look in the doorway to see who'd spoken those words.

"I told you to go away," I said, refusing to look at him.

"I can't. You need me. And you may not like it, but I'm here to stay, so you'd better get used to it."

A chill traveled over my body as I looked into his clear blue eyes. I bet to anyone else he would be considered handsome and charming. But to me he was cold, calculating, and manipulative.

I pulled my cell phone out of my jeans and dialed Tave. "Auntie Tave, I have a problem. Can you come to Mom's room now? It's important."

I clicked my phone shut and looked up at the doorway— only to discover my father was gone.

Vanished. Just like that.

But he was still around. I could feel him.

Auntie Tave rushed in like an elfin tornado. "What's the matter? Is Liz okay?"

"No change so far. But Tave, she and the baby could be in real danger, and I'm not talking about the Bborim. Dad is back. He came by the house this morning and then was here just a few minutes ago. He says the hospital called him, but I think that's BS. I think he's been here for a while. I think Mr. Charles was telling the truth when he said my dad sent him after me. I'm scared that he's here to hurt Mom and the baby."

Octavia's face paled. "This isn't good. What did he say?"

"He basically said he knows he screwed up and he's here to make things right. That he knows we don't have anyone to take care of us and he wants to help."

"Okay, you're right to be suspicious, AJ. He's here for something. Or someone. He's not to be trusted. We need to have a family powwow. We can't leave your mom or the baby alone for even a second. Someone has to be with them at all times."

"Auntie Tave, there's something else. We found one of the runes last night. The rune is trying to communicate with me and tell me where the next one is. If things go well, we'll have the second one today. We think there are three in all, but we can't let Dad know about them. I think that's why he's really here."

My phone rang. It was Lex.

"Duffer's good. He completely lost us. No scent, no trail, nothing. He's a better magician than we gave him credit for."

"Where are you now?" I asked.

"Back at the house. We thought maybe he'd show up, but so far, nothing."

"I need you to tell Aunt D to bring the kids up as soon as possible."

"Everything all right, sailor?"

"No. I need you here, too. And bring the rune."

Chapter 16

Octavia made sure someone watched over Mom and the baby while we went to a private conference room for a meeting.

The whole family was there except for Ryan. Nobody had seen him since this morning, and he wasn't answering his phone or his 911 texts.

We all sat at a large oval conference table, with Octavia acting as family CEO. The twins were still wearing their pink plaid PJ pants and cheer camp shirts.

Oz had his nose buried in his Nintendo DS, while Rayden was looking over his shoulder, trying to be a backseat gamer. Aunt D had her knitting, but her face did not have its usual happy and relaxed expression.

I sat between Lex and Robbie. Lex reached over, taking my hand in his. The gesture warmed my belly and eased the worry and fear that had been weighing on my heart.

I was both mentally and physically exhausted.

"We've got a situation," Octavia started. "And everyone in this room needs to be made aware of how serious it is." Auntie Tave looked over at the twins, sadness clear on her face. "Girls, your father is back. And he's saying he wants to be involved with you since your mom and Rick are both out of commission right now."

Their eyes went wide.

"I don't even remember what he looks like," Ana said. "And I don't care, either."

Ainsley couldn't seem to sit still. She fidgeted in her chair, twisting her hands. I tried to reassure her with a smile, but she didn't meet my eyes.

"I know this is hard," Tave said. "But you two have got to stay away from him. You cannot allow him in the house. At all. Is that clear?"

"He's not a dichampyr or a Bborim," I said. "He was born vampire, so why does he need to be invited in?"

"When Liz and Rick married, I cast a protection spell on the house. Evil must be invited in, in order to enter the house physically. Obviously, I havna been able to keep them out mentally, but I'm working on that. 'Tis very important to keep everyone out of the house except for the people in this room. And, of course, Ryan. Where is that lad?"

"Right here," Ryan answered as he opened the door. "Sorry, my phone died. As soon as I recharged I got your messages and rushed over." He ruffled Oz's hair as he took the empty chair next to him. "Anyone care to fill me in?"

Octavia did a quick recap.

"If this is a family matter, why are they here?" Ryan asked, pointing at Lex and Robbie. "We have no idea if they're on our side or not. What if we've already invited the evil into our house?"

"That's enough, Ryan Fraser," Aunt D said. "Get yerself in check, lad. I understand yer concern, but we're a family. And we do this as a family."

"What if history repeats itself, Aunt D? What if these guys are somehow manipulating AJ? How do we know they're not working with the Serpentines? How do we know one of them isn't the Bborim?"

"Because they don't smell like maple syrup. And because when the Bborim tried to kidnap me yesterday, Lex and Robbie were there to save me," I said. "I wouldn't be here right now if it hadn't been for them."

I felt Lex tense at the mention of the demon, but only because I was holding his hand. There was no other outward indication that Ryan's comment bothered him.

"You were attacked?" Ryan asked, genuinely surprised.

I released Lex's hand and leaned forward. "I tried to call and warn you, but you wouldn't answer the phone. We were attacked trying to leave the church yesterday. Ryan, after everything we've been through, after last year's mess, do you really believe I would do anything to hurt my family? Our family?" I sighed. "Do you really believe I would do anything to hurt you purposefully?"

For the first time since the Bborim showed up in our lives, Ryan looked at me. I mean, *really* looked at me. His eyes softened and his face relaxed, and for a brief moment I felt him.

And I longed for him.

It was unsettling how quickly those buried feelings resurfaced.

"I don't want to believe it, AJ. But if we don't learn from our history, we'll repeat it."

"Ryan, ye're repeatin' it now. It wasn't a trust that split our clans, it was the lack of. If ye divide us, ye weaken us, and they win. That's all they want is a weak spot. One small blemish to prey on. And ye're givin' it to 'em, love."

Ryan's brows drew together as he processed Aunt D's statement. The idea that he might be the one who could cause history to repeat was a hard pill for Ryan to swallow.

When all was said and done, we'd worked out a body-guard schedule for everyone. Lex and Robbie took the first shift. Tave had arranged with Dr. Douglas to move Mom and Rick into the same room because of the special circumstances.

Rick had regained consciousness that afternoon and was no longer listed in critical condition. His vitals were looking exceptionally good for his condition, but we knew that was probably due in large part to a little special juice Aunt D snuck him.

Unfortunately for Mom, no amount of magic, in juice or woo-woo form, seemed to help. Every few hours they would run a CBC, and her hemoglobin and hematocrit levels were still low. (We vamps know what a good H&H level is. It's what we live for, so to speak.) The good news was that her levels seemed to be holding steady. The bad news was that they weren't high enough to get her out of the semiconscious state she kept drifting in and out of. She needed to start rebuilding her blood, stat. The transfusions were keeping her alive, but they weren't healing her.

Dr. Douglas met with Octavia and me privately to break the news. "I've been doing an extensive amount of research and I've determined the only thing that will save her is pure Serpentine blood."

"I'm part Serpentine—would that help?"

"We've been giving her part-Serpentine blood—we've even been giving her some of Lex's and Robbie's blood, since trainer blood tends to be a fast healant. The human in their blood was hurting her more than helping her. We can't explain it, but for whatever reason she has no vampire healing properties left. Right now, it seems all the vampire blood is disappearing from her system, so she's more human than vampire, and it's killing her."

"You guys have full Serpentine blood available to you, right?" I asked.

Octavia sighed. "Yes and no. It's rare to have it. Even more rare than AB negative is for humans. As you can imagine, the pure-blooded Serpentines aren't always the most open to giving their blood to save the impure."

"What are our options?"

Dr. Douglas scratched his five-o'clock shadow and

sighed. "We've ordered three units of Serpentine blood from the nearest vampire blood bank. It will be here this afternoon. Three units will buy us some time, but it won't be enough. She's going to need more—fast."

The heaviness that had been weighing on my heart just thickened. I'd been saying I would do anything to protect my family—did that include bargaining with the devil?

Could I ask my father to save my mother? Did I have a choice?

No. I didn't. But he did. He could say no. He could and probably would refuse. And where would that leave me?

Well, it would leave me motherless, that's where. As far as I was concerned, that wasn't an option.

Maybe Dr. Douglas was wrong. Maybe the three units would be enough to heal Mom. I hoped so, because I couldn't imagine depending on my father for anything— let alone help saving his half-breed ex-wife.

Lex was stationed with the parentals this shift, and Robbie was with Baby F. I opened the door to find Lex sitting in a chair between the beds, flipping the rune over and over, tracing the etched symbol. He looked lost in thought, so it startled me when he spoke without taking his eyes off the stone.

"Hello, sailor. Was wondering if I'd get to see you before you took off."

"You sure are concentrating awful hard on our little friend there. What's going on?" I asked, walking over to Mom. I leaned over the bed and kissed her cheek. She stirred, but didn't open her eyes. "Has she woken up at all?"

"Yeah, she's flitted in and out, but she's really weak."

"Can you read her thoughts?"

"I can, but she's so doped up, they don't make much sense. Really foggy stuff. Now, Rick is pretty good company when he's awake."

I smiled and looked back at Momma. She seemed so small and frail. And weak. I couldn't stand to see her like this.

"Any sign of my father?" I asked.

"Haven't seen him, but Robbie says he's here. Says he's felt Clive a couple of times while he's been watching the babe. He hasn't heard anything specific, but he feels him. At first he thought it was you, but he realized quickly that it was your dad. You two have a similar brain imprint."

The thought that I shared anything other than history and bad blood with my father made my stomach bubble. "You haven't felt him?"

"No. Robbie's the brain, I'm the muscle, remember?"

"You're fishing for a compliment," I teased.

"Maybe," he said, laughing. "I miss being in your head."

"I thought you liked a challenge."

"I thought I did, too. And speaking of a challenge—" He tossed me the rune.

As soon as I caught it, the sickly sweet smell of the Bborim burned my nose.

"What?" Lex asked when I wrinkled my nose in disgust.

"Can't you smell it?"

"No."

The rune warmed me like a sauna as I held it. I tried to ignore the gut-roiling smell and just concentrated on the stone. I opened up my mind like Robbie had been teaching me and sent out feelers into the world.

"Talk to me," I whispered.

The smell just got stronger. "The Bborim is in the hospital," I said. "I smell it. It's making me sick."

"Let me talk to Robbie, see what he says." Lex did his vampire mind-trick thing with Robbie. "He says no. It's not in the building."

"Then why do I smell it? It's here. It's trying to get into my head. Trying to see if it can learn where the next rune is. I need to find Ryan. We need to do this together, like we had planned."

"Let me call someone to stay with your parents and I'll come with you."

"No, Lex. I need you to protect my parents. Besides, if I expect Ryan to trust me, then I have to trust him. I'm going to give him this rune, and we're going to find the next one together."

Chapter 17

 drove straight home from the hospital, hoping to catch Ryan at the house. We had to get on this fast.

And I had to convince him to work with me. After the family meeting this morning, he'd agreed that we should all work together, but I could tell he was holding back. He was saying the words we all wanted to hear, but something in the way he said them told me that's all they were—words.

I pulled into the driveway, but Ryan's Jeep wasn't there. Would he answer if I called him? Probably not.

That overwhelming sweetness washed through me the moment I stepped out of the car and I had to stop myself from retching. It was here.

And it wanted what I had.

I had to get into the house.

The rune was a constant source of heat. It didn't burn through my pocket or anything, but it was definitely noticeable. And I was nervous carrying it around with me. The only source of protection I was wearing was the necklace Aunt D had given me last year. And although that had helped me while I was being stalked by the dichampyr, I had no idea if it was strong enough to keep a Bborim at bay.

Or my father.

Part of me just wanted to hide the rune in the house, where I knew it would be safe. But the only way I could convince Ryan to trust me would be to hand it over to him. Why couldn't he be at home, where we would be protected?

Because that would be too easy, that's why.

As I was unlocking the carport door, a car pulled into the driveway. I turned, expecting to see Ryan, but was surprised to find Malia instead.

I sighed in relief.

"Hey," she said, getting out of the car. "I was just at the hospital looking for you. Robbie said you'd come home. I'm so sorry about your parents."

"Hey, girl. I'm okay. Rick is doing well, the baby is doing well, but Mom is struggling. She's getting another transfusion today."

"Wow. That sounds serious," Malia said as she strode over to me. She opened her arms like she was going to hug me, then stepped back suddenly, her eyes wide. "Oh, sorry. I'm about to sneeze."

"That's okay," I said, and laughed as she fired off a series of achoos. When she finished the sneezefest, she walked with me to the door. And when I said walk, I meant hobbled.

"Are you limping? What's wrong with your leg?"

"I'm a longtime sufferer of graceitis. I tripped over my own two feet yesterday and banged up my leg pretty badly."

I finished unlocking the door and went into the kitchen, leaving the door ajar behind me. I opened the fridge, grabbed myself a "V8," and almost hid the rune in a carton of eggs. But no, I needed to take it with me to show Ryan.

"Have you got plans today?" I asked, my back still to the door.

"Yeah, Robbie and I are going to have lunch," Malia said from the carport.

I closed the fridge and turned around. "What are you doing out there still?"

"I just assumed you were grabbing something real quick and coming back out. You seemed in a hurry."

"Good call. I am in a bit of a rush. I need to find Ryan. You don't happen to know where he is, do you?" I asked, going back outside and locking the door behind me.

Malia's face darkened. "Yeah, he's at Bridget's. I actually went over there to see if she wanted to come with me to the hospital to see y'all. They were both a little shocked to see me. I swear they're up to something."

I shook my head. "They're working on extra credit for Mrs. Christopher."

"Convenient." She rolled her eyes. "Will you be up at the hospital soon?"

"Yeah. Right after I find Ryan. You and Robbie have been spending a lot of time together. You really like him?"

"He's so smart, AJ. And he makes me laugh. Plus, his lips are like—"

"Ugh. Really don't need that mental image, but thanks. Y'all have fun today; I'll see you later."

I drove straight to Bridget's house. I thought about calling first but decided against it, just in case.

Ryan's Jeep was parked in the driveway behind Bridget's car. Good. They were both here.

Ryan opened the door before I knocked. "Are our parents okay?" he asked.

"Same. Your dad is getting stronger, which is good. Mom is having another transfusion today. The docs say she needs pure Serpentine blood to heal her, but they don't think they have enough in stock."

"She'll be okay," he said. "I really believe that."

I could tell he did believe it, and that warmed my heart. "Thanks. I hope so. Listen, we need to talk," I said. "It's important."

"Can it wait? I'm in a hurry. I have to be somewhere in a few minutes."

"No, it can't wait. I'll just come with you."

I followed him to the Jeep, opened the passenger door, and hopped inside. I inhaled deeply, savoring the smell of leather and Ryan. He got in and started the car. "What's so damn important?"

"Take this." I handed him the rune.

His ears turned red, but other than that, he masked his surprise very well. "Is this what I think it is?" he asked.

I nodded. "What does it feel like to you?"

"It's warm. Like oddly warm. It feels almost alive," he

said, turning it over in his palm. "How strange is that?"

"Robbie was right," I said with a smile. "You're a key holder, Ryan."

He snapped his head toward me.

"You're my Frieceadan counterpart. And we have to work together to find the other runes. Is the stone telling you anything?"

He shrugged but didn't say anything.

"Ryan, just trust me. What do you see?"

Ryan immediately let go of his poker face as the wall he had built up came crashing down. He looked at me with soft brown eyes and sighed.

"When I shoved Lex this morning, I must've touched the rune in his shirt pocket, because as soon as I did, I could see the rune sitting in a glass case in the artifact room of the library. I tried to retrieve it with one of the spells Aunt D has been teaching me. I've gotten really good with my casting; Aunt D has been working with me a lot while you and Buffy have been training."

I giggled. "Have you been calling him Buffy in your head?"

Ryan sheepishly smiled. "Buffy the Vampire Trainer. From day one."

"No wonder he's digging at you every chance he gets."

He laughed. "Yeah, well, that was the silver lining to this whole thing."

"So you have the second rune, then?" I asked as he started the Jeep and pulled away from the curb.

"No. I went there this morning to try to get it, but I couldn't. The first time I tried, I was visualizing the location of the rune and tried to pop it into my hands but wound up literally popping the rune up into the glass case and shattering it. Which, of course, set off the alarm. Good thing I was outside the building and could get away before the sheriff got there. That would've been awkward. Anyway, that's where I'm headed now."

I reached over and touched his hand as he shifted. Warmth slowly spread from my arm to my chest to my belly. I swallowed, trying to wet my suddenly dry throat. "Then let's do this together."

He was quiet for a few minutes, and the tension between us thickened like gravy. I let go of his hand and stared out the window as he drove. Finally, he spoke.

"My feelings haven't changed, you know," he said, his voice gruff with emotion. "I've tried, but I can't seem to find the cure for you."

Every nerve in my body seemed to spark at his words. My heart quickened, my stomach knotted, and my fingers itched to touch him again. I wanted to scream, *Me too!* But I knew that was a bad idea.

"Ryan—"

"I know," he said, looking at me again with warmth in his eyes. Our gazes locked, and I knew right then that nobody would ever replace Ryan Fraser in my heart.

Ever.

I cleared my throat and changed the subject. "So, what's the plan?"

"Just go in and ask the librarian if we can please check out the ancient artifacts and assure her we know nothing about who vandalized the library this morning?" Ryan said with a smile.

"I think we might need a little bit more than that. You drive, I'll plot."

The library was about four blocks from our house, and I thought it might be a good idea if Ryan and I had a diversion. So I called Ana as we drove.

"Hey, Ryan and I need you to bring Ainsley and the boys to the library, ASAP," I said.

"Why?" she whined. "We were going back to bed."

"Ana, we're getting the second rune and we need your help. *All* of you."

When we got to the library, Sheriff Christopher's car

was still parked out front. Great.

"You must've done a helluva job breaking into the library with your fingertip fireworks, Ryan."

"I did my best to create as many problems for us as possible."

"Mission accomplished." I laughed.

We sat in the library parking lot and waited for the kids to arrive. It felt good to just sit in silence together, with no tension between us. Well, other than the elephant of sexual tension that was in the car. But we were going to ignore that.

Ana and the boys rode their bikes up to the bike rack and parked them.

"Where's Ainsley?" I said, getting out of the Jeep.

"She wouldn't come. She's been grumpy lately. I had to hunt her down in the tree house. She's been trying to keep me out of her head. I think Robbie's been giving her mind-blocking lessons on the side, because I've had a real hard time finding her lately."

"She's at the house, though. Right?"

"Right. She won't leave by herself," Ana said. "Mom's accident freaked her out. She won't even talk to Aunt D or Auntie Tave right now."

"We'll give her some space and I'll talk to her this afternoon," I said.

"So what's the plan?" Oz asked. "Do I get to use one of the new spells Aunt D has been teaching me? I can make the lights go out now."

"We might need that. We're definitely going to need a diversion."

While we planned our strategy, I couldn't help but feel uneasy. We were being watched; I could feel it. And that stupid smell was back.

"Do y'all smell something sickly sweet?" I asked, remembering that none of them had smelled the Bborim that day at the farm.

They all shook their heads.

"Well, I do. I'm not sure why I can smell that thing and y'all can't, but it means we're not safe right now. It's here somewhere. Watching."

We all entered the library together. Being a school day, it was empty except for Mrs. Horvath the librarian and Sheriff Christopher.

"Kids, what are y'all doing here? I heard about your parents; I'm so sorry. How are they doing?" Mrs. Horvath asked.

"Getting better. Mom is still in pretty bad shape, but she's trying to stabilize."

The sheriff came out of the artifact room with his

notepad. He smiled at us, but I saw the suspicion register in his eyes.

"I lost my cell phone the other day," Rayden said. "I think I left it here."

"Oh well, nobody's turned it in to the lost and found yet," Mrs. Horvath said.

"Can we look around?" Ryan asked. "With our folks in the hospital, we really need to be able to stay in touch."

"Of course, hon. Just don't go into the artifact room. We had some vandalism this morning and there's broken glass everywhere. I don't want you to get hurt."

We all nodded.

The sheriff and Mrs. Horvath wrapped up, and the sheriff left.

"I'll be in my office. Come get me if you need me," Mrs. Horvath said, walking behind the circulation desk to her office.

"Mrs. Horvath, I'll come with you and look through the lost and found. Just in case," Ana said, following.

Ryan gave his little brother a high five. "Nice job, Rayden. That's a much better story than the extra-credit research crap we came up with. Like we'd really do home-work with our parents in the hospital. What the hell was I thinking?"

Ryan took over. "Rayden, hang out by the circulation desk and keep an eye on Mrs. H. We don't want her getting suspicious. Oz, come with AJ and me. We may need your help."

Oz's face lit up like a flashlight. "Sweet."

I could hear Ana talking Mrs. Horvath's ear off in the office, keeping her distracted. Rayden pretended to search for his "lost" cell phone, which he just happened to have in his pocket. And Ryan, Oz, and I headed toward the artifact room.

"Uh, you didn't tell me you used a pipe bomb," I whispered. The place was a mess. There was glass everywhere, old books strewn about, and even some of the artifacts were on the floor.

"I didn't do this," he said. "There's no way I did this."

"The demon did it," I said, finally realizing why I kept smelling it. "It's leaving a residue when it visits. I smell it before it arrives, and apparently I'm smelling it after it leaves. I know it's been trying to get into my head, too. I've had to work really hard to keep it out." I opened my hand. "Give me the rune and let's find its mate."

The stone hummed to life in my hand. I realized now that every time I practiced opening myself up to the senses around me, I was also opening up my mind to outside forces. So I focused hard on keeping my wall strong while I tried to be receptive to the rune's message. "The stone is still here. The demon didn't get it. But it's buried under a pile of rubble."

"Okay, Oz, I need you to work your special magic," Ryan said.

"Turning the lights off?"

"Nope, not that trick. You're the best in the family at telekinesis. Start with the books. Can you stack them all up in a corner?"

"Sure."

I watched in awe as Oz just raised his eyebrows and with barely a nod managed to quickly pile up every book in the room into two neat stacks.

"Now the artifacts. Move them all to that empty shelf."

Pottery, jewelry, drawings, and other assorted artifacts just floated over to the shelf and gently landed there. Ryan carefully stepped through the remaining rubble to examine the items.

"Keep an eye out for me," he said.

"Any luck?" Mrs. Horvath called from her office.

"Not yet," Rayden answered. "I'm going to check the computer area. I was there for a while yesterday."

"Hurry, Ryan. I don't think we can buy much more time," I whispered.

"It's not over here," he said. "I've touched everything, and nothing is warm. Nothing is humming. It's not here."

I pulled the first rune from my pocket and concentrated again. "It's here. But it's still somewhere in the rubble. Oz, can you move all the broken wood into a pile and all the glass into another pile?" I asked quietly.

Oz shot me a look that said *duh!* This move seemed to require more effort than the last two. I guess since he was separating two different items, he had to concentrate a little more. He closed his eyes, lifted his hands, and before I could say "Cleanup in aisle nine," there were two separate piles of rubble. The floor was almost spotless now.

Except for the sand-colored stone sitting on the floor where the broken flowerpot had been.

As soon as Ryan touched the stone, a black etching appeared on the surface.

"Whoa!" Oz said. "Dude, how'd you do that?"

"This magic is way over my head, kid. Let's get out of here."

"Found it!" Rayden yelled from next to the computer stations once he realized we were leaving. "It must've fallen

192

out of my pocket over here. Thanks, Mrs. Horvath."

"You're welcome, guys. My love to your parents."

The kids loaded up on their bikes and headed straight to the house. Ryan drove me back to my car, which was still parked at Bridget's.

"Now what?" I asked, examining both stones. The rune I had found was an iridescent black, possibly carved from obsidian. Holding both stones was intense. They hummed loudly, and instead of a lingering warmth like before, it was a searing heat that had me sweating.

I focused on the stones to see if they would tell me where the final rune was located.

"All I can see is Mrs. Christopher," I said.

"Then I think that's where we need to go next."

"Let's take these home first. I want them to be safe. And if that thing is reading my mind, these aren't safe away from the house."

"Agreed."

As Ryan turned onto the old county road toward Bridget's subdivision, the demon smell filled my nose.

"Ryan, the Bborim is here. Somewhere."

The words were barely out of my mouth when we heard a loud pop and then another one. Ryan tensed his grip on the steering wheel as the Jeep heaved forward. He slammed his foot on the brakes but nothing seemed to happen.

"Hold on!" he yelled as the Jeep swerved left and he tried to pull it back to the right. I grabbed the "oh shit" handle and did my best not to think, *Oh shit!*

There was another loud bang and the Jeep jumped forward like we'd been hit from behind. I glanced backward, but there was nothing there.

Only a gray fog, and the sickly sweet smell left behind by the Bborim.

The tires were thumping now as tread flew off in large chunks. The Jeep didn't seem to slow down at all, even though Ryan was no longer giving it gas.

I heard him murmuring something under his breath and I knew he was working on a spell. I gripped the handle tighter.

The road exploded in front of us, creating a bathtub-sized crater and sending asphalt flying around us. Another explosion behind us sent more asphalt raining down. Panic now owned my body, and my heart was hammering like I'd just taken a hit of speed.

But Ryan never broke his concentration, and just before the Jeep took a nosedive into the crater in front of us, we lurched to a halt.

"Are you okay?" he asked.

I was shaken but not hurt. "Yeah. I'm fine."

"I'll call the sheriff and you call Bridget," Ryan said. "I'm not sure how I can explain the craters in the street, but I suppose that's really for them to figure out. Get Bridget to take you to your car, and then I'll meet you back home."

I pulled out my cell to call Bridget and then thought for a second. "Take one of the runes. It's obvious they want them, and they're going to do whatever they can to get them. I shouldn't have them both."

He nodded, holding out his palm. When I laid the warm stone in his hand, I was almost blinded by the burst of light in my head.

Our hands were connected and we couldn't let go. It was like the rune was supergluing us together. I looked at our hands, then up at Ryan's face. His pupils were dilated, making his dark brown eyes seem almost black. I couldn't break away from his gaze.

The seconds felt like hours and the air grew thicker. Slowly Ryan pulled me to him. When his lips touched mine, it was like a secret passed between us.

No, not a secret—a truth.

The kiss was warm and electric and everything a girl dreamed a kiss should be. It was more than just heat; it was filled with whispers of destiny that had my skin tingling and my head spinning.

And ringing. No. Wait. That was my phone.

I broke the kiss in a haze and answered my phone.

"Um, hello," I said. My voice was gravelly.

"Did I wake you?" Lex asked.

Guilt coursed through me when I heard Lex's voice. "No. I'm awake. What's up?"

"Your mum's not doing so well. I'm sorry, love. The transfusion of the Serpentine blood wasn't enough. They need more, but I'm afraid it's not looking very promising."

Worry and dread sat in my belly like an anvil. "I'm on my way."

I clicked my phone shut and looked at Ryan. Tears burned my eyes; I tried to blink them away, but one escaped. Ryan caressed my face and brushed the tear away with his thumb.

"I've got to go," I said. "It isn't looking good for Mom right now."

"I'll come with you," he said.

"No. Go to Mrs. Christopher's house and see if you can find the third rune. I'll call you if it gets worse."

Chapter 18

ridget picked me up and drove me to my car. She told me she'd been up to visit my mom a couple of times, which really touched me. We admitted we'd been missing each other like crazy and that life without your bestie was no life at all. But it was still a little tense between us. We promised that once everything settled down we'd try to get back to being us.

My life was a full bucket of hurt and confusion. My mom was dying. I could save her if I asked my dad for help, but it felt risky. Would he help? He said he wanted to be back in our lives; would he donate blood to my mother to prove it to us?

I knew I had no choice. I would beg him if I had to.

Either way, the man who had abandoned his family eight years before was my only chance at keeping the family together now.

Then there was the torn-between-two-lovers aspect of my life. Lex was everything a fantasy was made of. He was sexy, and fun, and made my toes curl every time he looked at me. And underneath his bad-boy persona was a really good guy.

But he wasn't Ryan. Which, when it came right down to it, was the most important ingredient.

Lex was a physical pull; Ryan tugged at my soul.

I guess I wasn't really so torn at all.

When I parked in my driveway, my heart jumped into my throat. Leaning against a carport post was my father.

He looked relaxed, like he was supposed to be there. Dread traced my spine, and I shuddered. He knew I needed him.

He approached as I closed the car door. "What are you doing here?" I asked.

"I think you know."

My throat was scratchy and my mouth dry. "You're Mom's only chance. Are you going to help her?"

"What's my incentive?" he asked.

"Your daughters," I answered, walking past him. He

made me nervous. I didn't want him near me. I didn't trust him. "I thought you wanted to make things right between us. Make up for abandoning us. Has that changed?"

Clive Ashe's smile was anything but friendly. "You're smarter than that, AJ. You called my bluff the moment I showed up. You know exactly why I'm here. You've known all along, haven't you?"

I couldn't hide my disgust.

"You're here for me," I said. "Mr. Charles was right last year—you sent him for me. You're the guy in the cloak, the guy in my dreams. You've been trying to manipulate me for months. And now you're using my mom to get to me. You're the reason she's in the hospital, aren't you? You did this to her—to us. Because you need me for something."

A wave of nausea hit me when he laughed. "You're a smart girl. A lot smarter than your old man, that's for sure. I moved the family here specifically to find those damn runes. I searched everywhere. My gut told me at least one would be hidden at the church, but I couldn't find any clues. Nothing. We had no idea who the key holders were. I could've been one just as easily as you. But I still disappointed everyone in the clan when I came home empty-handed.

"Now, if I would've taken you with me when I left,

I'd have been a hero. But hindsight is twenty-twenty," he said. "Yes. I do need you, and now, coincidentally enough, you need me. I'll give your mother the blood she needs, but you have to do something for me first."

"What's that?" I asked, even though I knew the answer already.

"The runes, my dear. You give me the runes, and I'll save your mother."

"Runes? I don't know what you're talking about." Maybe I could play dumb.

His ice-cold stare saw right through me. Unlike Ryan, I must have the world's worst poker face.

"You're a smart girl and a bad liar. Give me the runes or your mother dies."

Like I had a choice.

"Fine. Here." My hand shook as I took the stone from my pocket and handed it to him. Maybe the one would satisfy him.

He closed his eyes as he ran his fingers over the shiny sand-colored rune, then smiled. "I need the other one, too. The one you just found at the library."

Had he gotten into my head? Had he followed me? How did he know? "I don't have it. I purposefully didn't bring it with me just in case something like this happened."

I walked past him and unlocked the carport door. "You are *not* invited or welcome in this house. Let me make that very clear."

"I never thought I was," he answered, holding his hands up. "Let's talk about getting me that second rune."

Anger and shame boiled in my belly, but I had no choice but to follow his demands. I had just earned Ryan's trust. We were on the same path to protect our family. And now I was about to betray him to save my mother.

Ryan would never forgive me for this.

I just made a bargain with the devil and sealed myself a new fate.

Chapter 19

I left Daddy Dearest and drove straight to Mrs. Christopher's.

"AJ! I'm so happy to see you! I'm terribly sorry about your parents. Al is working overtime to find the other vehicle involved. How's your mom?" Mrs. Christopher asked when she opened the door.

"She's not doing so well. Needs more blood."

"I'm a universal donor; I'll be sure to donate for her this afternoon."

"Thanks, Mrs. Christopher. Is Ryan still here?"

"He's actually upstairs in the library doing some research. Before you go up there, could I grab you for a minute? I'd love for you to help pick out some artifacts that the Art Department will be using as inspiration for the prom decorations. I've had the worst time narrowing them down."

Mrs. Christopher led me down the hallway. "We're going to the second room on the left. It should be the spare bedroom, but it's turned into my own personal Valley Springs Museum. Al finally broke down and removed the bed for me. It was just in the way."

She opened the door to the bedroom, and immediately I felt like I had stepped into a museum vault. The room was full of pottery, jewelry, old furniture, drawings, and paintings.

"Wow. This is amazing."

"It really is. I still marvel at what great condition some of this stuff is in. If I hadn't had these checked out for authenticity myself, I wouldn't believe they were hundreds of years old."

Magic is *pretty amazing,* I thought.

"So I was thinking we could just go through some of these things and pull some pieces that had detailed etchings on them so the art guys could copy them for the murals. What do you think?"

"Sounds great to me. Where do we start?"

Her phone rang. "Let me go get that. Just start pulling

anything out that you think would make a good decoration. I'll be right back."

Where to begin? Hmm.

I glanced around the room and decided maybe I should begin with the pottery section. Maybe the rune was hidden in a bowl or something.

The collection of pottery was extensive. Probably a hundred pieces, most of them in almost pristine condition. I picked through the assortment, checking the inside of every piece that had a lid. No rune. I pulled out a few items that had some very distinct etchings on them. Thought they would make some pretty cool decorations.

I had probably been on my own for about fifteen minutes when Mrs. Christopher returned. Her usually chipper demeanor had been replaced with a much more somber look.

"I've got some bad news. It seems like our prom theme may be getting nixed because of 'parental concerns.' I've got to go meet with the principal and the parent who filed the complaint now."

"I bet it's Mrs. Ledbetter. Cathy has been going on and on about witches being all about the devil. She's so stupid. I've been tempted to just hit her in the head with a skillet."

Mrs. Christopher laughed. "I think we should make a list of people who deserve a skillet to the head. Like people who do self-checkout at the grocery store with a basketful of stuff."

"Oh my God, yes! Or people who let their dogs crap in your yard and then don't clean up."

"And clowns. All clowns should be hit with skillets," Mrs. Christopher added.

"Clowns deserve a skillet to the head, then Tasering," I said with a laugh. "Good luck with your meeting. I wasn't the biggest fan of this prom theme, but now that we're doing it, I'm kinda into it. Plus, it's really too late to plan anything new. The prom is next week!"

Mrs. Christopher nodded in agreement. "You and Ryan are welcome to stay. Mr. Christopher will probably be home in an hour or so. I'll call and let him know y'all are here. And if you're gone when I get back, I'll call you and let you know where we stand on a prom theme. We may have to have an emergency prom committee meeting if things don't go my way."

"You sure it's okay if we stay?" I asked.

"AJ, what are you guys going to do? Steal from the town sheriff? I don't think so." She winked. "Just keep pulling out stuff you think the art guys can use and hopefully things will go as planned."

As soon as Mrs. Christopher left the house, I ran up the stairs to the library and explained the situation.

"Hey. I heard you downstairs. So we have free rein right now?" he asked.

"Yup. For at least an hour. So we need to get busy."

We decided to focus most of our attention in the museum room instead of the library. It didn't make much sense to us that the rune would be hanging out among a bunch of books.

Ryan picked up a necklace and examined it. "I know the rune is here. It's weird. The moment it was in my hand, I just kept seeing Mrs. Christopher, and instinctively I knew that meant she had the third rune."

"Well, I suppose it makes sense that she'd have it, since she is a descendant of one of the original families. Is she Frieceadan as well?"

"No, she's all human. She might have some latent abilities, but her bloodline is pretty much all human now."

"Does she know about you?" I asked, opening a wooden box with some pretty amazing etchings on it. I felt around the bottom and discovered a hidden compartment holding some old recipes, but no stones.

"No. Because she's such a scholar in all things Valley Springs, she knows my family tree goes all the way back to the first settlers as well. But I get the feeling she thinks the magic was more exaggeration than actual magic. Which works for us."

My cell phone buzzed in my pocket, and I flipped it open to see a text from an unknown number:

I'm waiting.

Guilt coiled in my gut as I tried to figure out how to get the second rune without making Ryan suspicious.

"I've been thinking," I said. "Do you think it's such a good idea to have the stone here? In an unprotected house?"

"Oh, good call," he said, sounding a bit surprised. "Wow, that thought never occurred to me. Man, I'm gonna make a great warlock one day with this awesome brain of mine."

"Shut up. Anyway, I need to go back to the hospital and check on Mom. Why don't you keep looking for the third rune and I'll take the second one back to the house for safekeeping."

"Sounds good to me." He pulled the black stone from his pocket and without hesitation gave it to me.

He completely trusted me.

And I was about to betray him, just like he suspected I would a few days ago.

"Take it."

He sealed his trust with a kiss, and my heart was lost.

The man formerly known as Daddy was waiting for me in my car. I didn't say a word, just pulled out the rune and handed it to him.

"We're going to the hospital now," I said. "We're still looking for the third rune, so until we find it, you're going to keep up your end of the bargain."

The rest of the weekend was fairly uneventful. Ryan never found the third rune, but as long as I made an effort to keep looking, my father kept supplying my mother with blood. He and I met with Dr. Douglas privately to make arrangements for the donation. I knew I couldn't tell Auntie Tave about where the blood came from. Dr. Douglas agreed to say he had found an anonymous donor on his own so she wouldn't ask questions.

Guilt ate at me like an ulcer, but every day that Mom improved, I told myself I had done the right thing.

Besides, my dad had only two of the runes. My one consolation in this whole thing was that if Ryan and I couldn't find the third rune, then chances were Clive Ashe wouldn't be able to find it either.

As long as I looked for the third rune, he would

continue to go to the hospital and donate blood. If I refused, so would he. Dr. Douglas said Mom needed four or five days of the pure-blood transfusions, but it looked like they were working.

So every day I went to Mrs. Christopher's house under the ruse of prom decorations and searched for the third and final rune.

I didn't search very hard, but I *did* search.

On Monday morning, I was getting ready to leave early for school to help Mrs. Christopher when I saw Ainsley making her way toward the tree house all alone.

"Hey," I said. "What ya doing?"

"Nothing. I've just really wanted some alone time lately, and this is the only place I can get it," she said, not looking at me.

"This whole thing has really freaked you out, huh?" I asked, putting my arm around her. "It's okay. It's all going to be okay." I wasn't sure I actually believed that, but I had to do my best to convince my baby sister that I did.

"Thanks. It's just been weird. All this stuff with Mom and Rick, and then doing cheer without Ana. I hate watching her sit on the sidelines and wait for me. It sucks, but she has to come with me because of that stupid demon. I'm just tired of always having someone with me."

"Is that really it?" I asked. "Because you and Ana go everywhere together anyway, so that doesn't seem like something you'd really be bothered with."

She shrugged. "Wayne likes her. He comes to cheer practice with her. And they sit on the sidelines and laugh and giggle the entire time."

"That must be the boy who helped her with her crutches the other day. I guess you always had a thing for Wayne?"

"Maybe," she said, looking like she'd just lost her puppy.

"I'm sorry, Ainsley. This really does suck. You know it will get better, though," I said reassuringly.

"No, it won't. Not anytime soon. Although I guess it helps that she's blocking me from her thoughts almost all the time now. At least I don't have to listen to her endless chatter about him now."

"C'mon, I'll take you to school a little early. She can ride with Ryan today. And if you want, I can ask Oz to zap Ana with some green boils like he did Mr. Charles. They're only temporary."

"Maybe Oz could do something to Wayne—you know, since he deserves to be punished for picking the wrong twin."

"Good call. We'll plot in the car."

After the incident in the Jeep (which was ruled a freak underground pipe explosion), Aunt D had supersized the protection spells on all the cars. We were all carrying bouquets of protective herbs in our backpacks, and she added protective crystals to our jewelry.

This danger was stronger than she'd ever encountered before, so she was struggling with trying to find the right approach on how to keep us safe.

I dropped Ainsley off at school, drove to our local Starbucks knockoff, picked up two iced coffees, and headed to school.

I arrived at school early so I could help Mrs. Christopher carry the collection of artifacts and books to the art room. She was already in her classroom, but she was in a meeting with Mrs. Grimm. The look on Mrs. Christopher's face told me this was not just a "good Monday morning" visit.

I stood away from the door, queued up my super-duper hearing, and listened in.

"Sarah, I'm sorry, but Mrs. Ledbetter has filed a formal complaint, so we're meeting with her today to try to convince her that this is not the best course of action to take."

"Mrs. Grimm, I really think the Ledbetters are just blowing this out of proportion."

"I agree, but if she pursues this, then you'll need to be prepared to go a different route for the theme. I'm telling you now so you can be prepared. You might want to have a couple of backup ideas in mind, just to be safe. The meeting is in an hour. I think you should join us."

"Good morning, AJ," Mrs. Grimm said as she left the classroom. "I'm glad to hear your parents are doing better. And congratulations on your baby sister. Does she have a name yet?"

"No, ma'am, not yet. We're just calling her Baby F right now."

I walked into the room. Mrs. Christopher was picking through the boxes of artifacts and sighing.

"Mrs. Christopher, you ready to take those down to the art room?"

"I'm afraid we may have to put a hold on this for a while. There's a complication."

Mrs. Christopher explained the situation and told me about Mrs. Grimm's "intervention" with Cathy Ledbetter's mom.

"Do you think we're going to be forced to change the theme?"

"I don't know. I hope not. The students are really looking forward to dressing up and having a nontraditional prom. And we're getting some regional exposure from a Memphis paper that called me for an interview. So this could really drive up tourism for the town. The meeting is in an hour, so we'll know by fourth period."

And the movie guy's voice rang in my head: "Stay tuned for the dramatic conclusion of *Vampire Wars: The Battle for Prom* after these messages."

Chapter 20

Bridget met me at my locker between third and fourth periods.

"Where's Malia? I haven't seen her all morning," I said.

"Not her keeper, you should know that by now," Bridget said. "So are you and Sexy Lexy going to the prom together? Because if you're not, I know half a dozen girls who would volunteer. Actually, they'd probably all pay to go with him."

"Hah. I'm sure. You know, he asked, but with all the drama going on at home, I probably won't go. It's just too much of a hassle, you know?"

"Seriously? It's our senior prom—you have to go!"

"Yeah, we'll see."

Bridget and I parted ways. I was almost to Mrs. Christopher's class when my stomach started to roil. The smell just came on so fast and so strong, I seriously almost hurled in the hallway. I leaned against a row of lockers and took a deep breath.

Thank God I didn't blow chunks. I don't know if there's anything more humiliating than having the janitor toss some vomit litter on your mess while the whole school looks on.

"You okay?" Malia asked as she walked up. She reached out to grab my arm but then pulled back. "You look a little pale."

"Do you smell anything?" I asked.

"Uh, nothing but the gourmet soyburgers we're gonna get for lunch. It makes me wanna vomit, too."

"Heh. Yeah. I'm fine. It's passed." I stopped using the lockers as a leaning post and stood upright. "Where were you this morning? Bridge and I waited for you at the lockers."

"Sorry. Meant to tell y'all I had a dentist appointment today."

"Oh, and how was old Dr. McKitchens? Does he still pass that one drop of spit between his upper and lower lip?"

"Ugh, yes! Thank God he finally put on a mask. I just wanted to grab my bib and wipe his mouth for him."

When I entered Mrs. Christopher's class, I could tell the meeting had gone well.

Mrs. Ledbetter decided to let it go, since she was the only parent who seemed to be remotely concerned. So now we could move forward with the current theme.

That was the good news.

The bad news came shortly after class started when Sheriff Christopher showed up. As soon as Mrs. Christopher saw her husband, I could tell she knew something wasn't right.

There had been a break-in and someone had ransacked the Christophers' home. Which was pretty ballsy, if you asked me—he was the sheriff, after all.

But I supposed a demon really wasn't very scared of a little old sheriff.

It didn't take long for the rumors to spread like wildfire that it was somehow connected to the Ledbetters' prom protest.

I knew it wasn't the Ledbetters. I just couldn't figure out how the demon or my daddy broke into their protected house.

My suspicions were confirmed when I walked out to

216

my car after school to find Clive waiting on me. "What do you want?" I asked.

"You know exactly what I want. And until I get it, I'm done giving your mother what she needs."

I had been waiting for this. "You make me sick. You have two of the runes and you know the location of the third one. I've kept my end of the bargain."

He smiled. "I want the third rune, and you're going to help me get it."

"If you couldn't find it, what makes you think I can? And how did you get into their house without an invitation?"

"If I had looked for it, I would've found it. But I can't seem to buy myself an invitation anywhere, so I had that stupid oaf ex-teacher of yours look for me. I'm really glad it doesn't take a rocket scientist to pick a lock."

"Mr. Charles?" I asked.

"I own him. Especially after his screwup with you last year. And since that stepbrother of yours gave him the green boils from hell, he's been pretty useless to me all week. But nobody needs to see him for breaking and entering. And my pet demon stayed very close to the house to keep him in line."

I shuddered. My father was a real piece of work. "How

am I supposed to find the rune?"

"Your boyfriend is going to help. Get in, and let's go to the hospital."

He moved out of the way so I could open my door. "Aren't you going to invite me in?" he asked sweetly.

It took all of my strength not to scratch his eyes out right there. "Please, join me," I spat.

He laughed as he sat in the backseat. I glanced into my rearview mirror to watch him close the door, wink, and disappear.

"Surprised?" he said with a laugh. It was creepy how I could hear him but couldn't see him.

"Nothing you do surprises me. You're despicable."

"Call your boyfriend."

Which boyfriend? I had to assume he meant Lex. Nobody knew about Ryan and me, and there was no way I was going to let him know about us. And frankly, once Ryan realized how I had betrayed him, there would be no more Ryan and me.

So I dialed Lex.

"There she is. If I didn't know better, I'd think you were avoiding me."

"Never," I said with a nervous laugh. I glanced into the rearview mirror with my eyebrows up. I had no idea what I was supposed to say.

"Tell him you think you know where the third rune is but need him to help you find it," the backseat said.

I did as I was instructed and added, "I'm on my way to the hospital. Can you leave now?"

"Sure. Rick's awake and doing well. He doesn't need me here to babysit anymore. And your mum is really starting to get stronger."

"Really?"

"She woke up today and was lucid. They think just a few more transfusions of the Serpentine blood and she'll be back to normal."

My heart sank. I was hoping he would tell me that she didn't need any more Serpentine blood so I could tell Daddy of the Year to get bent.

But no. I needed his blood, and the only way to ensure he would keep helping my mom was to find that third rune.

"I'll be there in ten minutes. Meet me out front?"

"See you there," he said.

I hung up the phone, a mix of emotions fighting inside me. "How do I know you're going to keep your word if I find the rune? How can I trust you?"

"You can't, I guess. But since I'm your mom's only

hope, I don't think you have a choice. Doc told me today they need at least two more donations, so for your mother's sake, you better hope you find that rune."

Lex got into the car, leaned over, and kissed me softly. I was a little tentative, trying to figure out how I could tell him I was distressed without tipping off the invisible dad in the backseat.

He pulled back with a strange look on his face. I smiled at him, hoping it came across as warm instead of whacko. Because at the moment I felt very much out of my mind.

"You all right, sailor?" he asked.

I nodded as I drove away from the hospital. Maybe I could open the door up to my brain and let him into my thoughts?

Wait. No. If I opened my mind to Lex, would I be letting Dad in as well? If Dad knew I was letting Lex in, he would stop helping Mom. And if Lex realized Dad was in the car, he wouldn't help me.

I was definitely caught between a rune and a hard place.

"Is this some top-secret mission that you can't tell me about in advance?" he asked. "You haven't said two words since you picked me up."

"Sorry. Lost in thought," I said. "So the second rune

has been showing us Mrs. Christopher's house as the location of rune number three. But we can't find it."

"And neither did the person who trashed her house," Lex added.

I shot him a look. "What makes you think that wasn't just someone trying to make a point about the prom?"

"I think you're being watched and that person realized there's a reason you're continuing to go over to Mrs. Christopher's house."

"Oh. Well, I guess that makes sense. But you don't think they found the rune?"

"No. Why else would we be heading that way now? The second rune is still talking to you, aye?"

"Um, yeah. That's right. So, anyway, I think Mrs. Christopher has a secret room or a safe, and I think the rune is in there."

"And you want me to read her mind to figure out if your hunch is right?"

"You're one smart kitten."

I parked in front of Mrs. Christopher's house. When I got out of the car, I looked into the backseat just to see if there was any hint of my father. All I saw was backseat. I started to walk away, but something in the window caught my eye.

Breath.

My father had leaned forward and breathed onto the window, then drew a smiley face.

Hmph. Still there.

Lex was watching me as we walked to the front door. "You seem a little off center today," he said. "I think we need another training session this afternoon. Are you up for it?"

"Sure. Actually, yeah. That would be great. I could use the stress relief." And that was definitely the truth.

I rang the doorbell, and Mrs. Christopher answered almost immediately. "Hey, you two," she said with a smile. "C'mon in. I'm just straightening up."

"We came to see if we could help," I said. "Did they do any real damage? Was anything stolen?"

"It looks like everything is fine. Two pieces of pottery were broken, but it looks like nothing was stolen."

"That's good. I can't believe someone would do this," I said. "Did they mess up your library upstairs?"

"Yes, I haven't even started in there. It's a disaster."

"Show me the way, Mrs. Christopher, and I'll do it," Lex said. "Libraries and I go way back."

"Upstairs, first room on the right. Thank you, Lex."

Please God, let him find the rune. My mother's life depended on it.

Two hours later, we were back in the car. The museum room was almost back to normal, and Lex did a pretty good job on the library.

But neither of us found the rune.

"Did you get any indication of a secret room? Or a safe? Or maybe a safety-deposit box?" I asked, my voice sounding desperate. "Please tell me you have a lead."

"Sorry, love. Nothing. The only thing Mrs. Christopher thought about was cleaning up the mess and trying to get past the violation."

"Why does the rune keep showing us Mrs. Christopher if that's not where number three is?"

"It's still showing you Mrs. Christopher?"

I nodded.

"I don't know then. Let's go home, get a good workout in, and, when Robbie gets home tonight, have him take a look at the runes. He's got a gift with that type of thing. He'll figure it out."

I glanced into the rearview mirror. He was there, watching, listening, and waiting for me to screw up.

"Sounds like a plan. If we can pull him away from Malia. Those two seem to be attached at the tongue nowadays."

I couldn't see the man in my backseat, but I could feel

his smile. He was enjoying this a little too much.

My stomach churned. On top of everything else that was going on, now I had to figure out how to keep Robbie and Lex from realizing the runes were no longer in my possession.

This was going to be very messy.

Chapter 21

ex worked me like a junkyard dog for the rest of the night. We played crouching tiger, hidden vampire for at least five hours.

And I have to say, I schooled him at least seventy percent of the time.

"Good job, sailor," Lex said as we entered the house. "I didn't get inside your head once. I'm impressed."

"Thanks." I walked into the kitchen, grabbed two hemoshakes, and tossed one Lex's way. "I'm glad we trained tonight. I needed it."

"Everything better now?"

"It will be after a shower and a full night's sleep," I said with a laugh. I drained my hemoshake and grimaced again.

"I really wish I hadn't gotten a taste for the real thing."

He laughed and held out his wrist. "I'll let you have another go if you want."

Tempting. Oh, so tempting.

I pushed past him to head to the stairs, and he grabbed my hand and pulled me to him. "I've missed this," he whispered as he kissed me. Guilt burned my stomach. "Are we still on for prom?" he asked.

"Yes. Unless you've changed your mind." It wasn't like I could take Ryan.

"No. I think it's the perfect way to say good-bye."

I pulled back and looked at him questioningly. "What do you mean, 'say good-bye'?"

"Robbie and I are leaving Sunday. We've been assigned to a new client. There's really nothing left we can teach you at this point, so consider yourself trained."

"But," I stammered, searching for the words. "What about—" *Us?* That would be hypocritical of me. "The rune? What about the third rune?"

His smile was sad. "You have all you need to find it."

I was torn between relief and sadness. He was making this easy on me. He was ending things for me, to ease my guilt. I swallowed the lump in my throat and stroked his cheek with the back of my hand. "Sexy Lexy is most definitely one of the good guys."

"I'm not the one for you, sailor. I knew the first time I was in your head. And the first time I was in duffer's. I wanted to be wrong, but there's no denying it. You guys might be complicated, but you belong together."

A tear slipped down my cheek. At one time I had thought so, too.

Robbie never came home, giving me a Get Out of the Tangled Web Free card. At least for one night.

Actually, if I planned the next couple of days perfectly, I could probably avoid Robbie altogether. I couldn't afford to let my guard down around him; he was too good at being a brain stealth. Since he and Lex were "moving home" again, they were no longer going to school. All I had to do was make sure I planned my hospital visits when they weren't on duty.

"Good mornin' to ye, dearie," Aunt D said when I entered the kitchen. "Ye no sleepin' well? Yer mum is healin' up quite nicely now, so ye should be restin' easier."

"I'm fine. My dreams aren't going away. I keep seeing myself getting crowned queen in front of a blood-covered crowd. The good news is, it feels like a real dream and not like someone is in my head manipulating me. So my training has worked—I'm keeping them out of my head even in my sleep."

"Is there some bad news, then?"

"Yeah. I'm worried the dream is an omen."

I sat at the bar with my hemoshake. Aunt D set a warm loaf of fresh baked bread in front of me. I tore off a hunk and slathered it with honey butter.

"My gram could always tell when I was carrying the weight of the world on my shoulders. She said I looked constipated. Lookin' at ye now, I know exactly what she was talkin' about."

I shrugged. "I'm fine. This has just been a stressful week, that's all."

"Aye, it hasna been easy. But I'd bet my cauldron it's more than that, lass." Aunt D took my hand in hers. "Trust is the answer. I've been telling Ryan to trust you, but do you trust yourself?"

I tried to blank out my expression when I looked at Aunt D. She smiled. "If ye can't trust yerself, ye need to trust those around you. The burden is easier to carry when ye have help."

"I'm going to the hospital before class," I said as I was leaving. "Can you and Ryan get the kids to school today?"

"I'll take the weans. Ryan left early to visit his father, so ye may run into him as well. Remember what I said, dearie. Sharing the burden may not be easy, but it is simple," she said with a wink.

I walked out to my car, opened the door, and tossed my backpack into the passenger seat. It landed with a thud and an *oof.*

Chills raced across my skin as I watched my father reappear, holding my backpack.

"You're leaving awful early this morning," he said.

"Have you been watching me? You're such a creep. I'll be so glad to be done with you."

"That's why I'm here. Find that rune today or I'm done. No more blood."

"You can't do that! You gave me your word."

His laughter was as cold as his eyes. "Circumstances have changed. Find the rune or your mother dies."

He put my backpack on the floor and got out of the car. "Oh, and one more thing. Baby F might be safe while she's in the hospital, or when she's in your house—but she won't be safe on the drive home. So find the rune and not only save your mom but, as a bonus, you can save that half-breed sister of yours, too. See how nice I can be?"

"Your benevolence astounds me."

He laughed and shut the door. I started the car and, as he walked away, I thought about running him over. The image of him flying off my hood as I sped on by put a smile on my face. I backed up, never taking my eyes off him as I quickly checked off the pros and cons.

The pros had it. I punched the gas and aimed my four-wheel killing machine at his back.

And he disappeared.

Bastard.

I had no idea if he went left, right, or up. Oh well. I would have to be satisfied with my fantasy version of his hit-and-run.

The drive to the hospital was becoming second nature for me, like getting out of bed to go to the bathroom in the middle of the night. I didn't have to look where I was going; instinct alone carried me there.

I hadn't been lucky enough to see Mom awake yet, but Lex, Ryan, and Auntie Tave assured me that she had been up and lucid, if only for a brief amount of time.

Baby F was doing well. She'd been moved to the regular nursery, and all the nurses were in love with her. They were even collecting a list of names for her and trying them out. Apparently, Baby F liked being called Baby F the best.

I always checked on her first. She was so tiny, and that hair was so black. She was beautiful.

And in danger.

This whole thing was my fault, and now it was even worse.

I turned away from the nursery to head toward Mom's room and nearly ran into Ryan. It was the first time I'd really seen him since the day of the accident.

"Hey," he said, brushing my hair away from my face. "I've been missing you."

"Me too," I said as the guilt bubbled in my gut. "I was just on my way to see Mom."

"We need to talk first," he said. "Your mom's asleep right now, anyway. C'mon."

He grabbed my hand and led me to the same conference room we had had our family powwow in the week before. He closed the door behind us and locked it.

I walked to the table, but Ryan pulled me back to him. He pressed me to the wall, and my heart skipped as my stomach burned.

"I need you to hear me," he said, touching his lips to mine, "when I tell you I trust you."

He breathed his truth into me with his lips on my lips, his palm to my face, his dark gaze piercing my soul.

My heart splintered like it was made of glass.

I fell into his eyes, savored the kiss, and tried not to choke on my guilt.

"Ryan." I broke the kiss and pushed him away. "I'm so sorry."

"AJ, I *need* you to hear me. I trust you. I know something has happened and that you're eaten up with guilt. I know you're afraid I'm going to walk away. I promise, that will never happen again. No matter what you tell me. I'm here to stay. I'm yours."

Chapter 22

I was surprisingly calm as I told Ryan about my betrayal. I knew he believed he wouldn't leave, and maybe that made it easier for me. I wouldn't hold him to his promise, of course. Even though he had every intention of staying, when he discovered the depth of my betrayal, he wouldn't be able to stop himself from leaving.

How could he?

And strangely, I was at peace with that. It sucked tainted blood, but I'd get over it. Eventually. Hopefully.

My heart sank as I finished my tale. Ryan's face was summer-storm black. His eyes were no longer dark-chocolate pools I wanted to swim in. They were granite. Just like the set of his jaw.

I bit my bottom lip and braced myself for the wrath of a lifetime. I deserved every word he would fling at me. I had betrayed his family, his trust, and put the world at risk.

I had sacrificed the lives of many to save one. I was no better than my dad.

Ryan stopped looking through me and finally looked at me, causing me to flinch. He blinked away the rage, put his hand over mine, and said, "I would've done the same thing. You had no choice. But Clive Ashe's control of you ends now. We're going to fix this together, and I know how."

I sighed deeply as relief and surprise washed through me.

"How?"

He picked up the receiver on the conference room phone and dialed. "Dr. Douglas, this is Ryan Fraser. Can you meet me in the conference room on the fifth floor? It's an emergency."

It wasn't much more than five minutes before Dr. Douglas arrived. "Oh, hello, AJ. I was going to call you in a few minutes. The donor hasn't shown up today. And your mother's starting to get weaker. He's usually here by now."

"That's actually why we called you. He's no longer going to be donating blood."

Dr. Douglas's face went grim. "We haven't seen as strong a response from the pure Serpentine blood as we had hoped. Cutting Liz off now will be detrimental."

"We're not cutting her off; we're just saying that snake's blood is no longer an option. I've been doing some research and I think I have the answer," Ryan said. "According to one of the old texts in Mrs. Christopher's library, there was a documented case very similar to ours. The difference was that the mother was a Frieceadan and the father a vampire. The child was a vampire, and the pregnancy was really hard on the mother. She was at death's door until they gave her blood from both a vampire and a Frieceadan. She had to have both blood types to survive."

My heart was so full. Not only was Ryan sticking around, he was also going to do everything he could to save my mother. "Will my blood work?" I asked.

"Our blood together will work. I know it. We have to save our family, AJ. Together," Ryan said.

"Let's do it," Dr. Douglas said. "We've got nothing to lose."

Four hours after the transfusion, I was sitting next to Mom, holding her hand and having a discussion.

Baby F was wheeled in a few minutes later, and my mother laughed until she cried. Rick was out of the bed and holding the baby faster than a hummingbird feeds. He took her to Momma, and they cooed and oohed and awwed over the little miracle they had brought into the world.

"What have you been calling her?" Mom asked.

"Baby F," I said with a laugh.

"Baby F with her jet-black hair and clear blue eyes. I can't believe I have a black-haired daughter."

"I can't believe I have a sister," Ryan said. "We're Frasers—we only have boys."

"I think we need to come up with something a little more definitive than Baby F, little girl," Rick cooed.

"Let's go," I whispered. "We need to give them some alone time while Mom is still awake."

We said our good-byes and left the room together. I realized once we were in the hall that the entire time we had been with our parents, our pointer fingers had been interlocked.

"We have a lot to figure out before they get home," I said, pulling his hand up to my lips and kissing his palm.

"It'll be complicated but worth it."

We left the hospital together, and he walked me to my

car. I started to open the door, but something in the air told me we weren't alone.

I squeezed Ryan's hand, took a deep breath, and called my dad out. "I know you're here. So just show yourself."

His laughter sounded before he appeared. He was leaning against the hood of the car, his hands folded across his chest, his feet crossed at the ankles. He couldn't have been more at ease if he'd just gotten a massage and taken a Valium.

Tension radiated from Ryan's body. I squeezed his hand again to rein him in. "I've got this," I said.

"It's obvious you needed a proper father figure, AJ. You know it's inappropriate to date your brother. Even for Mississippi."

"Yep, a proper father figure would've been good growing up. You should've thought about that before you left. Now, get off my car; we're going home."

"How's Mommy? I bet her breathing is getting more and more shallow by now."

"Actually, no. She was sitting up, holding the baby, when we left. She no longer requires your services."

Anger flashed across his face, but he cloaked it pretty quickly. "I still require your services, Daughter."

"I'm no longer your daughter, and I'm also no longer

your go-to girl for the third rune. If you want it, you're going to have to find it yourself. Now, if you'll excuse us, we missed school today, so we have to get our make-up work."

Ryan and I got into the car. I tried not to be smug as I started the engine. It felt good to tell that asshole off. He may have donated his DNA to me, but I was nothing like my father.

"I hope you can live with your decision," he said.

I rolled down my window. "It's over, Dad. Mom is healing, the rune is still hidden, and I'm no longer under your control. The family knows about you, and Aunt D is working on a new batch of ju ju that will protect the baby until she gets home. So why don't you take Mr. Charles and your pet Bborim and get the hell out of our lives."

I burned rubber as I pulled away.

"Wow," Ryan said. "That was *hot*."

Chapter 23

The rest of the week went by in a blur of school, homework, and prom plans—and no sign of the Bborim, Dad, or Mr. Charles.

Lex and Ryan buried the hatchet, and not even in each other's back. Robbie was completely preoccupied with Malia, so he never seemed to be around anymore. Aunt D had cooked up some super-duper magic that included our entire property and our cars, so dear old dad couldn't sneak up on us again.

I had gotten really good at detecting his presence, though. Lex said I had far exceeded their training, that my natural abilities were stronger than any he had ever seen. He encouraged me to think about becoming a trainer.

Ryan didn't think that was such a good idea.

Everything seemed to fall into place. Mom and Baby F were going to be released on Sunday if everything stayed the same. Rick was released Friday, but he refused to leave their sides. Not that I blamed him.

The only thing that still felt out of whack was Bridget. Technically, we were okay with each other, but it still felt a little forced. It was the only thing left that really weighed on me. Somehow I had to patch the friendship between her and Malia. Or I just had to stop hanging out with them both together. That thought made me sad, but if it would get me back the whole Bridget, I would do it.

Sure, knowing my dad had two runes was a concern, but since the third was safe from him, the sense of urgency was gone. We would fix this—we just didn't have to do it tonight.

I was kind of excited about the prom theme, now that the day was here. I was going to get to let my fangs down and walk out in public with my head held high.

That would be very cool.

Well, it would be cool if I could figure out what the hell I was going to wear. With everything that had gone on these past few weeks, a prom dress had been the last thing on my mind.

Since I was going to be a vampire, I didn't have to go the traditional route. But looking through my closet, I realized I didn't even have anything to work with, even for a nontraditional outfit.

I would start with the shoes and work my way up. If I had to do an emergency shopping trip, so be it.

I pulled out a pair of pretty damn badass thigh-high black boots that I rarely got a chance to wear. I had a black miniskirt and a hot pink minidress that might work. I pulled them out of the closet, just in case. Maybe Aunt D had a cape or something I could borrow.

I grabbed the boots and the skirts and ran downstairs. Aunt D was in the kitchen as usual, whipping up something divine while rocking out to ABBA.

"Hello, dearie," she said between lyrics. "Are ye hungry? I'm baking a meat pie, if ye can wait a few more minutes."

"No, thanks. Actually, I was wondering if you happened to have a cape or something I could borrow for tonight. I never bought a dress and I'm trying to throw an outfit together now."

"Och! I canna believe I forgot to tell ye. I have yer outfit all ready to go. It's in my room—let's go try it on."

"How did you know?"

"I wish I could take credit, but it wasna my idea. That Lex is somethin' else, he is. Came to me a few days ago with the thought that you might need somethin' to wear. I didn't have any idea what a proper vampire should wear to a vampire ball, so he gave me some specifics. Told me what he was wearin' and what he thought ye'd like. I was skeptical at first, but I think the boy was right."

We walked into her apartment. She clapped her hands and the lights came on.

The outfit was hanging on a closet door. I got closer to examine it, and my words failed me. "Wow."

"Before ye get too excited, try it on."

I stood in front of the full-length mirror and put the final touches on my makeup.

Aunt D worked her magic on my hair. It was now curled in long ringlets and pulled up in a fancy coif with a blue satin ribbon woven throughout. I stood back and admired myself.

Holy smokes.

Lex might be a good guy at heart, but he was still a guy. I not only looked like a vampire, I looked like a vamp.

The outfit wasn't a dress, exactly. The top was a black

fitted bustier. Aunt D said Lex had requested strapless (of course he did), but she thought it best to cover my chest, shoulders, and arms with a sheer black material that reminded me of panty hose. You know, so I wouldn't "catch a cold." The neck was lined with blue piping that matched the ribbon in my hair.

I wore leather pants that were so fitted they felt like a second skin. But they were also stretchy, like my favorite pair of yoga pants. My thigh-high boots looked kick-ass with them.

My favorite part of the outfit was the detachable skirt that was open in the front so I could showcase the boots and pants. It was kind of like a cape for my ass. Its color depended on the light and angle. If I turned one way, it was the same color as my ribbon. If I turned another, it was black with blue shimmers.

This outfit was made of awesome. And I was pretty confident I looked good enough to eat.

My suspicions were confirmed when I walked down the stairs to find both Ryan and Lex waiting for me, drooling all over their tuxes and tails. Lex wore a top hat, and his tie was the same color as my ribbon.

Ryan was wearing a wine-colored cloak over his tux, and he carried an old cane made from a Rowan tree.

"I knew you'd wear that well," Lex said, tipping his hat to me.

"You're bad. You did this on purpose." I laughed.

"I don't know what you're talking about," Lex replied with feigned innocence.

"I can tell you one thing," Ryan added. "There's no way in hell you're going to prom without me. You've got two dates tonight. Or one date and one bodyguard. However you choose to look at it."

"So which one of you is the bodyguard?" I asked.

"Not it!" they replied at the same time.

"I guess that means I have two dates. Let's go, fellas."

Chapter 24

I hadn't helped decorate because of all the madness, so I was genuinely surprised to walk in and see how amazing everything looked. There were large murals of old stone buildings, wells, a kirk, and even a real stone circle.

Thousands of twinkling lights hung from the ceiling, making it feel like you were outside on a cloudless night.

Ryan leaned in and whispered, "I may have helped the decorating along just a little bit."

It honestly looked like we had gone back in time. Amazing.

Most everyone, including the teachers, dressed up. Witches, warlocks, wizards, vampires, and a couple of creatures that I'm pretty sure were from *Star Trek*. But whatever, everyone was in costume and having a great time.

"Have you talked to Robbie tonight?" I asked Lex.

"No. I haven't seen him all day. I'm sure he's stuck to Malia's face somewhere. I swear, that lad loses ten IQ points every time she's around."

"Have you talked to Bridget?" I asked Ryan. "I need to talk to her—I really want my friend back. All the way back."

"She's over there," he answered. "With Grady."

Bridget looked gorgeous, wearing a forest-green velvet dress and a shimmery silver cloak. "I decided on witch," she said when I walked up to her.

I smiled, showing my fangs. "Vamp."

"The outfit gave that away. Damn."

"I know, right? I can't even talk about how sexy and weird I feel. I'm almost ready to change back into my blue jeans and flip-flops."

She laughed a little and then got quiet. The silence stretched out between us for a few moments, and then we both tried to talk at the same time.

"I'm sorry," we said.

"Me too," we said again.

"I realized last night that me being upset with you over Malia isn't fair to you. We've been pulling you in the middle of our fight all year, and I know that hasn't been easy. I promise to try harder with her." The pained look on her face told me she would try but she wouldn't necessarily like it.

I nodded. "And listen, I've got some stuff I have to tell you. Things haven't been right between us because I've been scared to tell you the truth."

"Can you tell me now?" she asked.

"No. Not here. But I will. I promise. If you promise me that you'll listen and remember that I'm still me. No matter what I tell you, I'm still me."

Bridget gave me a funny look, then smiled. "Promise. Are we friends again?"

"Never stopped being friends." We hugged, and relief flooded me. Telling her that I was a vampire wasn't going to be easy, but in my heart I knew she would eventually accept it.

"Let's boogie." She grabbed my hand and pulled me onto the dance floor.

The night seemed to be going amazingly well. Everyone was dancing, posing for pictures, laughing, and having an all-around good time. For the first time in two weeks, I was relaxed and enjoying myself.

Lex and I danced a lot, as we had to continue the facade that we were a couple. Ryan and I hadn't worked out the details on our reemergence as a pair. It might be better if we waited until school was over to go public. No matter what we decided, we couldn't go public at the prom—not before we told our parents.

"Did you ever find Robbie?" I asked as Lex and I were slow dancing to some song that was sappier than a pine tree.

"Yeah, he and Malia came in while you were talking to Bridget. He was acting a little off, though. I'm serious; I think she sucks a little bit of his brain out every time she kisses him. He's never been this bad off before."

"We girls sometimes have that effect on you boys."

"Yeah, yeah. I'm thinking about staying for a while, now that I've seen you in this. Ryan needs some competition."

I smiled. "In another lifetime, maybe. But in this life, there is no competition for Ryan."

"I'm gutted. Seriously wounded. You know that makes me want you more, right?"

I stood on my toes and planted a kiss on his cheek. "I know. That's part of the fun."

He laughed loudly. "I may never get over you, sailor."

"You'll get over me. I'm thinking probably about day two of your next assignment," I joked. When he didn't laugh, I looked up to see what had his attention. He was staring off into space, concentrating like he saw something—but there was nothing there.

"You know, I can't find Robbie anywhere. In my head. He's gone. He was there, he was snogging Malia, and now he's completely silent."

"Go find him. I'll see if I can find Malia."

I was making my way through the crowd, looking for her, when Mrs. Christopher's voice came over the speakers. "Boys and girls, may I have your attention, please. It's time to crown this year's king and queen."

This was my least favorite part of the prom. Why did we have to go through this every year when, no matter what the occasion, Tiffany Talbot always won? And my guess was that since Lex was the sexy new guy, he'd probably win king.

That would actually be kind of fun to see—Lex in a tiara.

I kept milling through the crowd looking for Malia, but I wasn't having any luck. Mrs. Christopher was still talking away, but I had pretty much drowned out her voice while I concentrated on finding my friend.

"AJ. Did you hear me?" Mrs. Christopher asked.

I stopped when I heard my name and looked around to see the entire crowd staring at me.

"I'm sorry?"

"You've been voted in as queen this year. I suppose vampire queen would be the appropriate title. Come on up and wear your crown."

Me? What? Who was king?

And that's when I realized Ryan was onstage, wearing his crown and smiling.

Somebody had done a little more than help decorate last night. Somebody had used his very special powers to rig an election.

I made my way to the stage, trying to stamp down the nervous butterflies in my stomach. Finding Malia could wait for just a minute. Why was I so excited about this?

Because every girl wants to be Cinderella just once. And tonight, I was getting my chance.

Mrs. Christopher was beaming. She pulled a beautiful silver tiara from a velvet-lined box. There was a giant opalescent stone in the center, with smaller versions of the same type of stone on each point.

"Congratulations," she said.

I bent down, and she set the crown on my head. The

moment it touched me, a familiar humming began and warmth filled me from head to toe.

"Mrs. Christopher? Why didn't we see this at your house?"

"It's from our family collection. My sister brought it to me today. She lives in Memphis."

"Your sister? Your *twin* sister?" I asked, finally realizing why we kept seeing Mrs. Christopher's face but couldn't find the rune. It wasn't Mrs. Christopher after all.

"Why, yes, how did you know?"

"Just a lucky guess," I said with a laugh.

The DJ queued up the music, and Ryan took my hand and led me to the dance floor. The crowd parted, giving us plenty of room.

"You look beautiful," he murmured.

"As much as I want to revel in this moment—and believe me, I want to—we have a problem, Ryan. The third rune? I'm wearing it. It's in the crown."

"No shit."

"We need to get it out of here before Dad figures it out."

Out of nowhere, the sickly sweet Bborim b.o. hit me. "Ryan, the demon is here somewhere. We have to get the rune out of here!"

"AJ!" Bridget said as she rushed up to us. "Crap. I'm sorry to interrupt, but I just saw Malia with Mr. Charles. He was wearing a disguise, but I know it was him. And when Malia saw me, she took off like a bat out of hell."

"Where's Mr. Charles?" I asked.

"He's still here, but AJ, there's something else. You might think I'm crazy, but when he smiled at me, his eyes flashed red and I saw fangs."

"He's been changed," I said to Ryan. "Nobody's safe, Ryan. Not while he's here."

Bridget stared at me for a second, speechless. "Oh my God. That's what you need to tell me. That's what you tried to tell me last year. You're a vampire, aren't you? You are really a vampire."

"I am. And I can't wait to tell you all about it, but not now. We need to find Lex and Robbie."

Chapter 25

We found Lex pulling Robbie out of the janitor's closet. His hands and feet had been bound, his mouth duct-taped, and he was groggy, like he had been drugged.

"Is he okay?" I asked.

"He will be. Your girlfriend has done something to him. Drugs, probably, but I'm not sure. That would explain why he's been off center lately. And why I haven't been able to access his thoughts."

"The demon was here," I said, wrinkling my nose in disgust. "It's left that rancid sweet smell everywhere. Is it possible that Malia could've been somehow charmed by the Serpentines?"

"No," Robbie said with a raspy voice. "Not drugged."

"What, then?" Lex asked.

"Some kind of spell. I need my strength so I can figure it out."

Ryan's cell phone rang. I helped Robbie to a chair and grabbed a cup of punch from a passing underclassman. "Here, drink this."

As Robbie was trying to regain his strength, I scanned the crowd. I needed to find Malia and see if we could snap her out of this spell. But instead of my friend, I saw Mr. Charles skulking through the gym.

"Lex, we've got a problem. Mr. Charles is a newborn. He might be under his master's control right now, but we can't count on that."

"Let's go put some of your training to work, sailor."

I looked for Ryan, but he was still off on the phone. "Bridget, stay with Robbie?" She nodded as Lex grabbed my hand and rushed me into the throng of people.

As soon as Mr. Charles saw us, he ran for the back exit. But he wasn't running very fast.

"Why is he running? Why isn't he at least trying to use some of his vampire powers?" I asked.

Lex doubled over, shaking with laughter.

"Because he's not a real vampire," Lex said between guffaws.

We caught up to him in a matter of seconds. He turned and hissed, then flashed his fangs at us.

One of the incisors fell to the floor.

"Oh. My. God. Not only are you so desperate to be a vampire that you're faking it, but you're not even faking it well!" I yelled. "And is that a kilt? Are you wearing a kilt? Morris, Morris, Morris. Kilts are for real men."

"I am a vampire!" he insisted, his red eyes bugging out. "Look at my eyes! I'm just waiting for all my powers to come in."

"Dude. One of your fangs just fell out," I said.

He started to run toward the door, but I jumped and planted my kick-ass boots into his back, knocking him to the ground. His kilt came up around his waist. I was very relieved to know he was wearing boxers.

Glow-in-the-dark Halloween boxers with little vampire faces all over them.

"I've called the sheriff," Lex said. "Dracula here will be hauled off to the funny farm tonight."

I was still giggling when Ryan joined us, looking grave. "AJ, we have a bigger problem than this tool. Ainsley just called. She didn't go into details, but somehow she managed to let your dad into the house and he took Oz. He's kidnapped my baby brother."

I took the crown off and removed the stone from the

center. Sure enough, on the back surface was an etched symbol.

"Work your magic and replicate the stone. Then let's go get our brother."

I knew exactly where my dad had taken Oz: the abandoned farmhouse at O'Reily's.

We left Lex to take care of Mr. Charles and instructed Bridget and Grady to take Robbie to the house and make sure Aunt D knew exactly what was going on.

Then Ryan and I took off for O'Reily's.

"We need a plan," I said. "We can't just expect to trade the stone for Oz, and we can't let them have all three runes, so what are we going to do?"

"You know I've been doing loads of research, right?"

I nodded.

"I have a plan. I know it will work, but I need you to trust me. Do you promise you'll do whatever I say, no questions asked?"

"Yes. Anything."

"Okay, let's go kick some ass. And I have to tell you: I really hope I get a chance to punch your dad. What a prick."

"As long as I get my licks in, too."

The ten-minute drive seemed to take forever. Ryan drove to the back entrance of the farm and parked.

"Are you ready?" he asked, removing his cloak.

I unsnapped my ass cape, leaned in, and kissed him. "Let's do it."

We followed the path into the woods, and I used my super senses to detect any possible lurking danger. But nothing jumped out at us. I honed my senses, searching for my dad, but was unable to find any trace of him in the woods.

A flickering light glowed from inside the dilapidated building, and I saw my father standing in the window. Watching. Waiting.

Even though it was pitch-black in the woods, he saw us coming. His arrogant smile all but glowed in the dark.

"Here we go," Ryan said. "I need you to follow my lead."

We stepped into the clearing together, holding hands. He was still carrying the walking stick, and it suddenly dawned on me that it was much more than a costume prop.

He tapped the stick to the ground three times, then drew a ring around us while chanting a spell in Gaelic.

I know this was the wrong time to think it, but, damn, it was sexy.

He pulled out a small glass bottle that contained a white powder and herbs and sprinkled it along the circle and repeated the chant. Or maybe it was a new chant. I had no idea, because it all sounded the same.

"Isn't your brother cute. Or would that be boyfriend? I'm so confused," my dad said as he walked out, carrying Oz by the scruff of his neck. Oz's brown eyes were wide with fright, and his lips were set in a pale, thin line.

Ryan paid him no attention, just continued chanting and sprinkling.

"That's not going to do you any good, you know. It may keep you safe, but it won't do anything for your brother here since he's not in the circle."

"Dad, just let him go. You don't need him. I have the rune. If you'll let him go, it's yours."

"How can I trust you'll keep your word?" he asked, throwing my words back at me.

"I'm nothing like you, that's how."

"Touché. But if it's all the same to you, I'll keep my little insurance policy. Besides, I'm a little thirsty, and I haven't tasted preteen blood in forever. It's a delicacy."

I thought that would at least make Ryan pause, but

it didn't. He just continued to do whatever it was he was doing.

"Oz," he finally said. "Do you remember Rayden's favorite trick?" he asked.

Clive laughed. "I love sibling double-talk."

Oz nodded, his brown eyes growing wider.

"Now!"

Oz stamped, clapped, and spoke something unintelligible.

And nothing happened.

It took a moment for the nothingness to register with Clive, but when it did, he nearly choked himself laughing.

Tears rolled down his face as he loosened his grip on Oz and doubled over with laughter.

And Oz ran.

When Dad finally regained some control over himself, he wiped his face and looked up to realize that Oz had taken advantage of the moment and was now standing in the circle of protection.

"Sometimes the best tricks have nothing to do with magic, asshole," Ryan said.

I was starting to enjoy our little victory, but the demon's smell slammed into me like a mallet. I looked around to see if I could detect it, and that's when I saw Malia coming from the woods and dragging Ainsley by the ponytail.

"Yeah, and sometimes the best plans are the backup plans," she said. "Hand over the rune, AJ, or I make your sister a midnight snack."

Chapter 26

I'm sorry, AJ," Ainsley said. "I didn't know. I didn't know Dad was bad. He was so nice to me. Nobody was talking to me while Mom was in the hospital. I was so lonely. And he was there. I didn't know."

Crap. This was a complication we didn't need.

"Ainsley, it's okay, honey. This isn't your fault."

"It's *all* my fault. I invited him in the house and he took Oz. And then Malia came over saying she had just escaped from Mr. Charles and needed to use the phone. So I invited her in, too." Her voice was cracking. "It's all my fault."

"No, baby. It's not. Just hang tight. We will get you out of this."

I looked at Ryan. I had no idea what his plan was, but I had to trust him. Trust that he would fix this. That we would fix it together.

"Dad?" Ainsley said. "Daddy, you said you were sorry."

A flicker of regret passed across his face, but he didn't respond. "Malia, this was not the plan."

"No, it was the backup plan—you just weren't in the loop."

His eyes flashed with anger. "Who planned this?"

"Who do you think? Your father. Your life is not your own, Clive. It never has been. From the moment you left that half-blooded Serpentine whore of yours and went back to the clan, he has owned you. He made sure we had it covered in case you screwed up. He's always said living with humans rubbed off on you. So far you've failed to prove him wrong."

"What happened to the real Malia?" I asked. I had to know.

"Oh, she's dead. I sucked her and her grandmother dry the night of the party at O'Reily's farm. And their blood has given me plenty of shifting strength. I just had to bide my time until I knew for sure you were the key holder. Weren't you even curious about me not coming into your house the other day? You've always invited me in before—but that day in the garage, you didn't. You know, you should've listened to Bridget. That girl's got good instincts. She made this very hard for me."

A wave of sorrow hit me like nausea.

"The night of the party?" My voice quivered. "So you were the one who turned Noah?" I asked.

"Guilty. Poor guy thought he was going to get lucky with me after *you* left him high and dry in the woods that night."

Guilt burned my heart.

"And Robbie?" I croaked. "How did you manage to keep him in the dark?"

The demon who looked like Malia laughed. "I may not be able to cast spells, but being a demon does have some benefits. I drained his brain a little bit every time we were together. Not too much, because he needed to be easy to manipulate but still be functional."

"Tell us what you want, *Malia*, so we can end this," I said. Anger began to boil just below the surface. That demon would pay for what it did to my friends.

"Give me the third rune and I'll give her a head start," she said. "Half the fun is the chase anyway."

"No deal," Ryan said.

"You're cute. You really think this is a negotiation? Sorry, sport. That's the deal. You give me the rune and I'll give her three whole minutes. Or I'll spare her for you, AJ."

"If I ask, you'll spare her?"

She laughed. "No. I'll let her go if you'll come to me willingly."

I started to step out of the circle. There was no choice for me. I would gladly give myself up for my sister, but Ryan stopped me. "No. Follow my lead.

"Ainsley," Ryan said. "Listen. It's actually really good that you're here. I was going to have to call you anyway."

Ainsley was weeping quietly, but she looked at Ryan.

"Listen, sweetheart. I don't know if you're aware of your special talent, but you have one. And I need your help."

"I'm going to bite her if you keep talking to her," the demon threatened.

"No," my dad said. "You're not. Even my father wouldn't want you to bite his granddaughter."

"Wouldn't I?" Malia said. Her eyes changed from the color of iced tea to the ice blue eyes I saw in my dreams. Dad couldn't seem to process what was going on.

"You're my grandfather?" I asked.

Malia shifted into her real human form. The steel blue eyes were there, the graying hair, the sinister smile. Grandpa looked like a meaner version of my dad. He laughed.

"Hello, Granddaughter. It's nice to finally meet you both. Now, why don't we go get your sister and we can all live happily ever after with your real family."

"Not a chance, Grandpa. So are you the one they call Elder?" I sneered.

"No, that was your father. But it was a title for show only. We would never let someone so incompetent be a real clan elder."

My dad seemed to be shell-shocked. "You've just been using me as your puppet."

Grandpa laughed. It was the coldest sound I had ever heard. "You failed us when you couldn't find the runes all those years ago. But don't worry; you've almost redeemed yourself. Even though you couldn't manage to get rid of that newborn half-breed menace to our society, you did get us the tools we need to rectify all the wrong in our past. So you're forgiven."

"I'm *forgiven*?" Dad said. "I gave up everything for you—including the woman and the family I loved. All I ever wanted was to make you happy. To earn your trust."

"You're a failure, Son. But you're getting better. Maybe one day."

Dad couldn't mask his anger

"Ainsley, I need you to concentrate," Ryan continued. "I know you think it's only Ana that you're tapped into, but it's not. You can tap into anyone or anything if you try—you're like a human GPS, and I need your help finding the runes. Can you picture them?"

She nodded.

"Close your eyes and think about locating one of them. What do you see?" Ryan said.

"It's dark. That's all I see. Darkness."

"C'mon, Harry Potter. What do you think you're going to do here?" Grandpa said.

Ryan maintained his composure and ignored the taunts.

"Okay, now focus. Pretend you're right next to the rune and that you're using your night vision. What do you see?"

"Fingers. I see fingers."

"That's all I needed," Ryan said. "You did good."

Ryan said something else in Gaelic, lifted his hands, and sparks flew from his fingertips.

"Ow!" my dad yelled, pulling his hand out of his pocket.

"And now we have two stones," Ryan said with a smirk, holding up the sand-colored rune. "Wanna go for three?"

My dad stood there, speechless, completely in shock.

But Grandpa flew into a rage and took on his demon form. Gray smoke and the smell of pineapple cotton candy surrounded us.

"Run to the circle, Ainsley!" I yelled when the transformation began.

Ainsley was like a deer in the headlights, staring, unmoving, as the demon took form.

"Ainsley! Run!"

But she didn't.

The demon picked her up like she was a rag doll. "You or the girl," it said to me in a monster's voice.

I stepped out of the circle, and the demon laughed as it brought Ainsley's neck closer to its mouth. "I lied."

It was drooling as it lowered its mouth toward her neck. My body tensed, priming itself to jump to her defense, but I didn't have a chance.

Dad beat me to it.

"I gave up everything for you!" he yelled as he shot like a bullet toward the demon. "But I will not sacrifice my daughters. Not anymore."

When Dad hit the demon, it dropped Ainsley. I flew to her, scooped her up, and brought her to the circle.

Ryan touched my shoulder.

"I have all three stones," he said. "I took a chance that your dad had one in each pocket, and while he was distracted, I snagged the last one."

"What do we do now?"

"We fight."

He gave the runes to Oz and told him not to leave the circle for any reason. Oz nodded, and he and Ainsley huddled together like they were trying to ward off frostbite.

The demon and my father continued to fight, but it was clear the demon was stronger. I had to wonder if a week of depleting his blood supply hadn't played a part in Dad's weakened state.

Dad picked up a large rock and bashed the demon in the head. While it stumbled backward a few steps, Dad ran over to the circle, slamming into the invisible wall of protection.

"We're not opening the circle for you," Ryan said.

"I'm not asking you to. AJ, can you forgive me?" he asked. The demon crouched, ready to attack again. "I was weak and wrong. You are stronger than I have ever been. And even if you can't forgive me, I need you to know I'm proud of you."

Those were his last words.

The demon pounced, crushing Dad beneath its weight. Dad bared his fangs and bit into the demon's flesh, but the beast was too strong and too fast.

With a quick flick of its hands, the demon snapped Dad's neck.

Dad didn't turn to dust like Noah did. But I watched as the life slowly faded from his clear blue eyes.

Tears burned my cheeks as my heart opened and forgiveness filled it.

How could I not forgive him? He gave his life to save my sister. To save my family.

"So touching," Grandpa said, his voice sounding as monstrous as he looked. "Daddy died for his daughters. I love a sacrificial lamb."

"You killed your own son," I said. "What on earth is worth sacrificing your own child?"

"The greater good," he said. "One life for the lives of many."

Ryan took my hands in his. "Remember, you do what I tell you, when I tell you, no questions."

"I trust you."

"Is Harry Potter going to work up some special magic?

This should be fun," the demon said.

Ryan began his chant, and the demon continued to pace around the circle.

"No matter what he does, you'll never be strong enough to defeat me. And I'll never go away. The protection will eventually wear out, or you'll eventually give up. Either way, I'll win."

Ryan's chanting never stopped. The air turned electric around us. Our hair stood on end, goose bumps popped up, and my heart began to race as adrenaline surged.

The demon grew agitated as it paced, roaring occasionally and trying to break through the circle.

The air began to sizzle and crackle with little bolts of lightning. Ryan's hands were above his head as he chanted, and his eyes were completely dilated.

Suddenly he looked at me, completely focused, completely at ease, and as he pulled me to his neck, he uttered two words that shocked me to my core.

"Bite me."

Chapter 27

Do you trust me?

Ryan's voice echoed through my head. Was that him in my mind or was that me remembering his words?

Do you trust me?

Yes. Without a doubt, I trust you.

And with that, I sank my teeth into his flesh.

Ryan never wavered from his spell, even with my teeth in his neck. Heat filled me, raced through me like soaring fever, but I held firm, sucking only what felt right and doing everything in my power to keep my venom sacs closed.

My body temperature continued to rise, but Ryan held me firm to his neck, so I continued.

And then he released me.

I looked at Ryan; he was glowing like an ember. "Do not let go of me," he said. "Do not let go of my hand. No matter what."

So I held tight to his left hand as a fireball formed in his right palm. His words seemed to nurture the ball, and it grew and grew until finally it was the size of a basketball.

The demon had stopped pacing and was now crouched in a defensive posture, ready to deflect and defend.

Ryan stepped outside of the circle, and the demon roared.

My palm was so sweaty from the heat, but I gripped his hand tighter than ever.

As Ryan threw the fireball, the Bborim pounced.

The two collided midair, and the fireball seemed to just disappear. The demon was unfazed.

It crashed into Ryan, and I gripped his hand so tight, I thought I heard bones crack. The force of the hit jarred us, but Ryan didn't fall, and I didn't lose my grip.

Ryan never wavered from his chanting, and as the Bborim pulled a claw back to swipe him across the face, Ryan lifted his free hand, called the walking stick from the circle, and tapped it on the ground three times.

The demon exploded into burning ash.

Chapter 28

"Whoa," Oz murmured, bringing me out of my stunned silence. "That was badass. Where'd you learn that, and can you teach me?"

Ryan chuckled, then drew me into his embrace. "Are you okay?"

I was overwhelmed with both relief and grief.

"It's over now," Ryan whispered. "It's over. We're okay. We have the runes. And we're together."

"Why did you have me bite you?" I asked, finally able to find my words.

"The stronger the bond between the two people casting the spell, the stronger the magic. I knew the demon would be impossible for us to beat separately, but with a united front of unbreakable trust, it didn't stand a chance."

"Me biting you was the ultimate show of faith?"

"Yes. For both of us. And the magic we made together proved that."

The magic we made. As cheesy as it was, I liked the sound of that.

"Ainsley, are you okay?" She was pale and wide-eyed, still sitting on the ground. She nodded but didn't say anything. I walked over to her, helped her up. "Let's go home. This has been one helluva night."

"A prom night to remember," Ryan said with a laugh.

"Or to forget, depending on your point of view."

The ride home was quiet. We were all a little shell-shocked, although Oz seemed more excited than anything.

Every light seemed to be on in the house when we drove up. We parked, and I helped Ainsley out and walked her inside with my arms around her. Oz ran in, yelling for Rayden.

"Dude! You totally missed it. It was awesome. Next time you have to get kidnapped so you can see how awesome Ryan is!"

"There'll be no next time, lad!" Aunt Doreen said, swatting his head. "Git ye inside and clean up. Ye tell your brother all about yer adventure after a shower. Go on." She was smiling, but that quickly faded when she saw Ainsley. "Oh, dearie. C'mere to Aunt D. I have the perfect tea to fix ye right up."

Ryan and I had barely let go of each other since we left the farm. I was almost afraid that if I stopped holding his hand, it would all go away. I didn't want to take that chance.

We heard voices in the living room and went in to find Robbie, Tave, Lex, and Bridget.

"Where's Grady?" I asked.

"I sent him home," Aunt D said. "I didn't figure we could talk about everything with him hanging around."

"Bridget has been brought up to speed," Auntie Tave said.

"I really wanted to be the one to tell you, Bridge," I said. "I'm sorry I didn't tell you sooner."

"It's okay. I wasn't ready to hear it anyway. But I'm ready now. To hear everything."

I finally let go of Ryan's hand and sat next to Bridget on the couch. We hugged, and everything felt right again.

"Crap! I almost forgot Mr. Charles! What happened?" I said.

"Sheriff Christopher had him carted off kicking and

screaming to the state hospital. The man never stopped insisting he was a real vampire and that his superpowers just hadn't developed yet. I almost felt sorry for him," Lex said, shaking his head. "Now I just feel sorry for myself—looks like I missed all the action."

"Poor Buffy." Ryan laughed. "Always a trainer, never a slayer."

"You crack yourself up, don't you?" Lex said with no animosity at all.

"Totally."

Robbie cleared his throat. "Em, I'm really sorry about Malia. I don't know what happened, but my lapse of judgment nearly cost this family everything."

"No, Robbie. It wasn't you. It wasn't any of us," I said. "They played a brilliant game, but we eventually outsmarted them. She admitted to using her super demon powers and basically sucking you stupid. You couldn't help that. We would still be looking for the runes if it weren't for you, so thank you. For everything. Of course, I hate to break the news to you, but Malia was really my grandfather."

Lex started laughing. "You snogged an old dude?"

"I need to go wash my mouth out with lye soap," Robbie said. "Or kill myself."

"All right. It's been a long week, and an even longer day," Auntie Tave said. "Let's go to bed. Your parents come home tomorrow—let's get some rest so we can be mentally prepared to fill them in on everything."

The sun was shining bright when I finally opened my eyes after a dreamless, sleep-filled night.

I glanced at the clock and couldn't believe it when I saw the time. I had slept past noon. I hadn't slept that late in forever.

I took my time showering and getting dressed. I was alone inside my head for the first time in a long time. The best part of it was that I didn't have to work at keeping people out; they just weren't there anymore.

And it was a blessed relief having my thoughts, dreams, and feelings all to myself again.

I got dressed, slipped into my flip-flops, and opened the door to head downstairs. And that's when I heard the baby cry.

"Mom?" I called out. "Momma, are you home?"

"We're in the living room," she answered.

I took the stairs two at a time and found everyone but Ryan and Aunt D in the living room, fawning over the baby. Mom seemed completely herself again. Her coloring was great, her bruising was gone, and her eyes were shining with happiness.

Rick sat next to her, looking the part of a proud papa, as Rayden and Oz held Baby F. Rayden looked a bit overwhelmed, but Oz seemed completely at ease. Ainsley looked back to normal. Relaxed and worry-free. She and Ana were piled up in the oversized chair with the laptop, checking out the prom pictures that had already been posted to Facebook.

"Why didn't y'all wake me?" I asked.

"We just got home a few minutes ago, and after your big night last night, we wanted you to sleep," Mom said.

"Ryan told us everything," Rick said. "We're so proud of you two," he said with a smile.

Ryan came up behind me and wrapped me in a hug. I tensed up. "Um, I guess you told them everything, everything?" I asked.

Mom and Rick both laughed. "Actually, the bite mark on his neck kind of gave it away," Mom said.

"Oh, yeah." I had totally forgotten the bite mark. I turned and inspected the two little holes. "Could've been uglier," I said. "These aren't too bad." And that's when I noticed the shock of white hair right above his ear. "Ryan, where did that white hair come from?"

"Oh, well, it seems that's where his birthmark is," Aunt D chimed in. "Your mark changes as you grow and learn. Ryan's changed last night when he cast that spell. No warlock of his age or experience has ever been successful with such complicated magic. Which is why I did a little diggin' this mornin'," she said. "Ye might want tae sit for this news."

Ryan and I sat in the love seat together. Worry clawed at my belly again, but I pushed it away. Nothing Aunt D could tell us would be as bad as what we had just survived.

"Baby F is a witch. I've tested her. She'll have some pretty special skills, it appears, but she's definitely not vampire. Therefore, Rick and Liz are not the chosen ones."

"Okay? So Baby F isn't the prophesied child. Does that mean you'll be having another baby, Mom?" I said.

"No. My body couldn't handle another pregnancy, so the doctor took care of that for me while I was in surgery. This baby factory is closed."

"So we went through all that for nothing?" Ryan asked. "I mean, not for nothing, but you know what I mean. Baby F wasn't the prophesied child, so all that stuff wasn't necessary. They had the wrong baby. They had the wrong family."

"Sort of," Aunt D said. "They had the wrong baby, yes, but not the wrong family. Just the wrong time."

"Maybe all the stress of the past week has made me slow, because I'm not getting it," I said.

"They didn't have the wrong family, just the wrong couple. One day, the two of you will have the prophesied child. You will have the baby whose blood will be their antivenom. Ye were destined to be together all along."

Wow.

"How do you know all this?" I asked.

"My big book. It tells me everything," she said with a laugh. "Actually, I called Mrs. Christopher. We managed to piece together some of the missing text from both of our old books." She pulled out a folded-up piece of paper. "I wrote it down so I wouldna forget.

A brother of magic, a sister of blood
Will form a bond that shan't be undone
A babe born to them will unite the clans
Forever together they will rule the lands

"There's more, but that's the important stuff. Ye two are destined."

"I guess this means we have permission to date now?" Ryan asked.

Mom and Rick looked at each other.

"There will be boundaries," Mom warned. "Just because you're going to have the prophesied child one day doesn't mean you have to start trying right away."

Lex and Robbie came in then. "Clive was dust when we got to the farm. We wiped the place clean and planted the protective herbs you asked us to, Aunt D."

"Good lads."

"Well, we're off now. Headed to London for a while," Lex said. "Sailor, you should really consider joining the training group. They could use a girl like you."

"I think I'll pass. Besides, fate has something else in mind for my future. Thanks for everything, Lex."

He smiled. "I should be thanking you," he said. "Now I know what I've been missing, and I have no intention of settling for less. You've set the bar high."

My cheeks warmed. "Whoever she is, she's a very lucky girl."

Robbie cleared his throat. "May I hold the baby just once more? I'm going to miss the little troll doll."

"Of course," Mom said.

Robbie was beaming as he lifted the baby from Oz's lap. "Good-bye, Baby F. I'm going to miss you, sweetheart."

"I guess this is as good a time as any," Rick said. "Would you like to know your sister's name?"

"Yes!" we all said at once.

"She seemed to like Baby F so much, we decided to go with Fiona. Fiona Ashley Fraser."

Fiona cooed. I guess she approved.

I felt the warmth of Ryan's hand as he took mine. I looked into his dark eyes and immediately found myself. This was where I belonged.

I love you.

His words were in my head. Strong, clear, and full of emotion.

Maybe love doesn't suck so much after all.

Acknowledgments

First of all, everything I said in the acknowledgments of *Bite Me!* still holds true today. Writing *Love Sucks!* was one of the biggest challenges of my life, because it happened during one of the highest moments of stress I've ever experienced. I couldn't have written this book without the support, love, and laughter of the people below.

Deidre Knight—you're not only the best agent in the business, but you're also one of the best friends a girl could hope for. I could say thank you a million times over and it wouldn't be enough. Thank you for believing in me. And the TKA supporting team deserves a big shout-out as well. I'm very lucky to call y'all family.

Kristin Daly—editor extraordinaire. You did it again. I am a better writer and a better storyteller because of you. I got very lucky having you as my first editor.

To my critique partners and friends Maria Geraci and Louisa Edwards: If I were going to have any more children, I would be obligated to name them in your honor. I would not have survived December 2008 or January 2009 without the two of you. Love is not a strong enough word.

To my BFF, Jennifer Paulus Bridgers: Thank you for everything. Not only did you help me get through this book, you helped me survive my life.

To my Thursday Girls, who always make sure my wineglass is full and my laughter is real: I am so glad to be home.

Momma, are you sick of me saying thank you yet? And I'll throw in a high five to my sweet daddy, who apparently has been bragging to all his poker buddies about me. Word gets around, old man. Remember that!

To Dana Belfry, Michelle Scheibe, and Naughty Kate Pearce for not letting me give up on anything.

Scott Smith—my awesome boss at SPP. This book would not have been written if you hadn't given me a week off from work so soon after I started. You rock like a hurricane.

As strange as it may seem, this book couldn't have been written without the music of Staind, Theory of a Dead Man, and Bruce Springsteen. Thank you for music that inspires.

On that note, I can't possibly thank Bruce Springsteen without adding a very special thanks to my friend Archie Stone for properly introducing me to the Boss. I can honestly say these are "Better Days" now.

To Ian and Rader, my sweet boys who grew into young men while my head was buried in my computer: Thank you for loving me, for doing the laundry, and for surviving on ramen noodles and Hot Pockets while I was temporarily insane. I love you both more than life, but you still need to clean your rooms.

And last but not least, to Mark Francis. Thank you for giving me sixteen years of marriage, for my two beautiful boys, and for bringing me home.